If Death Ever Slept

Also available in Large Print
by Rex Stout:

The Broken Vase
Prisoner's Base

If Death Ever Slept

By Rex Stout

G.K. HALL & CO.
Boston, Massachusetts
1989

Published in Large Print by arrangement with
Barbara Stout and Rebecca Stout Bradbury.

G.K. Hall Large Print Book Series.

Set in 16 pt Plantin.

Library of Congress Cataloging in Publication Data

Stout, Rex, 1886–1975.
  If death ever slept / by Rex Stout.—[Large print ed.]
     p.   cm.—(G.K. Hall large print book series) (Nightingale
series)
  ISBN 0-8161-4794-9 (lg. print)
  1. Large type books. I. Title.
[PS3537.T733I35 1989]
813'.52—dc20   89-2150

If Death Ever Slept

—1—

IT would not be strictly true to say that Wolfe and I were not speaking that Monday morning in May.

We had certainly spoken the night before. Getting home—home being the old brownstone on West 35th Street owned by Wolfe, and occupied by him and Fritz and Theodore and me—around two a.m., I had been surprised to find him still up, at his desk in the office, reading a book. From the look he gave me as I entered, it was plain that something was eating him, but as I crossed to the safe to check that it was locked for the night I was supposing that he had been riled by the book, when he snapped at my back, "Where have you been?"

I turned. "Now really," I said. "On what ground?"

He was glaring. "I should have asked, where have you *not* been. Miss Rowan has telephoned five times, first shortly after eight o'clock, last half an hour ago. If I had gone to bed she wouldn't have let me sleep. As you know, Fritz was out for the evening."

"Hasn't he come home?"

"Yes, but he must be up to get breakfast and I didn't want him pestered. You said you were going to the Flamingo Club with Miss Rowan. You didn't. She telephoned five times. So I, not you, have spent the evening with her, and I haven't enjoyed it. Is that sufficient ground?"

"No, sir." I was at his desk, looking down at him. "Not for demanding to know where I've been. Shall we try it over? I'll go out and come in again, and you'll say you don't like to be interrupted when you're reading and you wish I had let you know I intended to teach Miss Rowan a lesson but no doubt I have a good explanation, and I'll say I'm sorry but when I left here I didn't know she would need a lesson. I only knew it when I took the elevator up to her penthouse and found that there were people there whom she knows I don't like. So I beat it. Where I went is irrelevant, but if you insist I can give you a number to call and ask for Mrs. Schrebenwelder. If her husband answers, disguise your voice and say—"

"Pfui. You could have phoned."

Of course that left him wide open. He

was merely being childish, since my phoning to tell him I had changed my program for the evening wouldn't have kept Lily Rowan from interrupting his reading. I admit it isn't noble to jab a man when his arms are hanging, but having just taught Lily a lesson I thought I might as well teach him one too, and did so. I may have been a little too enthusiastic. Anyway, when I left to go up to bed we didn't say good night.

But it wouldn't be true to say that we were not speaking Monday morning. When he came down from the plant rooms at eleven o'clock I said good morning distinctly, and he muttered it as he crossed to his desk. By the time Otis Jarrell arrived at noon, by appointment, we had exchanged at least twenty words, maybe more. I remember that at one point he asked what the bank balance was and I told him. But the air was frosty, and when I answered the doorbell and ushered Otis Jarrell into the office, and to the red leather chair at the end of Wolfe's desk, Wolfe practically beamed at him as he inquired, "Well, sir, what is your problem?"

For him that was gushing. It was for my benefit. The idea was to show me that he was actually in the best of humor, nothing wrong with him at all, that if his manner with me was somewhat reserved it was only because I had been very difficult, and it was a pleasure, by contrast, to make contact with a fellow being who would appreciate amenities.

He was aware that the fellow being, Otis Jarrell, had at least one point in his favor: he was rated upwards of thirty million dollars. Checking on him, as I do when it's feasible on everyone who makes an appointment to see Nero Wolfe, I had learned, in addition to that important item, that he listed himself in *Who's Who* as "capitalist," which seemed a little vague; that he maintained no office outside of his home, on Fifth Avenue in the Seventies; that he was fifty-three years old; that (this through a phone call to Lon Cohen of the *Gazette*) he had a reputation as a tough operator who could smell a chance for a squeeze play in his sleep; and that he had never been in jail.

He didn't look tough, he looked flabby, but of course that's no sign. The toughest guy I ever ran into had cheeks that needed a brassière. Jarrell's weren't that bad, but they were starting to sag. And although the tailor who had been paid three hundred bucks, or maybe four hundred, for making his brown shadow-striped suit had done his best, the pants had a problem with a ridge of surplus flesh when he sat.

But that wasn't the problem that had brought the capitalist to Nero Wolfe. With his sharp brown eyes leveled at Wolfe's big face, he said, "I want to hire you in a confidential matter. Absolutely confidential. I know your reputation or I wouldn't be here, and your man's, Goodwin's, too. Before I tell you what it is I want your word that you'll take it on and keep it to yourselves, both of you."

"My dear sir." Wolfe, still needing to show me that he was perfectly willing to have sociable intercourse with one who deserved it, was indulgent. "You can't expect me to commit myself to a job without knowing what it is. You say you know my reputation; then you are satisfied of my discretion or you wouldn't have come. Short of complicity in a felony, I can keep a secret even if I'm not working on it. So can Mr. Goodwin."

Jarrell's eyes moved, darted, and met mine. I looked discreet.

He went back to Wolfe. "This may help." His hand went to a pocket and came out again with a brown envelope. From it he extracted a bundle of engravings held by a paper band. He tossed the bundle onto Wolfe's desk, looked around for a wastepaper basket, saw none, and dropped the envelope on the floor. "There's ten thousand dollars for a retainer. If I gave you a check it might be known, possibly by someone I don't want to know it. It will be charged to expense without your name appearing. I don't need a receipt."

It was a little raw, but there was always human nature, and net without taxes instead of net after taxes certainly has its attractions. I thought I saw two of Wolfe's fingers twitch a little, but the state of our relations may have influenced me.

"I prefer," he said dryly, "to give a receipt for anything I accept. What do you want me to do?"

Jarrell opened his mouth, closed it, made a decison, and spoke. "I want you to get a snake out of my house. Out of my family." He made fists. "My daughter-in-law. My son's wife. It must be absolutely confidential. I want you to get evidence of things she has done, things I know damn well she has done, and she will have to go!" He defisted to gesture. "You get the proof and I'll know what to do with it! My son will divorce her. He'll have to. All I need—"

Wolfe stopped him. "If you please, Mr. Jarrell. You'll have to go elsewhere. I don't deal with marital afflictions."

"It's not marital. She's my daughter-in-law."

"You spoke of divorce. Divorce is assuredly marital. You want evidence that will effect divorce." Wolfe straightened a finger to point at the bundle of bills. "With that inducement you should get it, if it exists— or even if it doesn't."

Jarrell shook his head. "You've got it wrong. Wait till I tell you about her. She's a snake. She's not a good wife, I'm sure she's two-timing my son, but that's only part of it. She's cheating me too. I'll have to explain how I operate. My office is at my home; I keep a secretary and a stenographer there. They live there. Also my wife, and my son and his wife, and my daughter, and my wife's brother. I buy and sell. I buy and sell anything from a barn full of horses to a corporation full of red ink. What I have is cash on hand, plenty of it, and everybody knows it from Rome to Honolulu, so I don't need much of an office. If you know anyone who needs money and has something that is worth money, refer him to me."

"I shall." Wolfe was still demonstrating,

to me, so he was patient. "About your daughter-in-law?"

"This is about her. Three times in the past year I've had deals ruined by people who must have had information of my plans. I think they got that information through her. I don't know exactly how she got it—that's part of the job I want you to do—but on one of the deals the man who got in ahead of me, a man named Brigham, Corey Brigham—I'm sure she's playing with him, but I can't prove it. I want to prove it. If you want to call that a marital affliction, all right, but it's not my marital affliction. My marital affliction is named Trella, and I can handle her myself. Another thing, my daughter-in-law is turning my home into a madhouse, or trying to. She wants to take over. She's damned slick about it, but that's what she's after. I want her out of there."

"Then eject her. Isn't it your house?"

"It's not a house, it's an apartment. Penthouse. Duplex. Twenty rooms. I own it. If I eject her my son will go too, and I want him with me. That's another thing, she's getting between him and me, and I can't stop it. I tell you, she's a snake. You said with that inducement"—he gestured at the bundle of bills—"I should get evidence for a divorce, but you don't know her. She's as slick as grease. The kind of man you were suggesting—one of that kind would never get her. It will take a man of your quality, your ability." He shot a glance at me. "And Archie Goodwin's. As I said, I know Goodwin's reputation too. As a matter of fact, I had a specific suggestion about Goodwin in my mind when I came here. Do you want to hear it?"

"I doubt if it's worth the trouble. What you're after is divorce evidence."

"I told you what I'm after, a snake. About Goodwin, I said I have a secretary, but I haven't. I fired him a week ago. One of those deals I got hooked on, the most recent one, I suspected him of leaking information on it to a certain party, and I fired him. So that—"

"I thought you suspected your daughter-in-law."

"I did. I do. You can't say a man can't suspect two different people at once, not you. So that job is vacant. What was on my mind, why can't Goodwin take it? He would be right there, living under the same roof with her. He can size her up, there'll be plenty of opportunities—she'll see to that if he doesn't. My secretary had his meals with

9

us, so of course Goodwin will. It occurred to me that that would be the best and quickest way, at least to start. If you're not tied up with something he could come today. Right now."

I didn't like him, but I was feeling sorry for him. A man of my broad sympathies must make allowances. If she was as slick a snake as he thought she was, and he should have been a good judge of slickness, he was out of luck. Of course the idea that Wolfe would consider getting along without me at hand, to be called on for anything from typing a letter to repelling an invasion in force, was ludicrous. It was hard enough to get away for week ends. Add to that Wolfe's rule against spouse-snooping and where was he?

So I was feeling sorry for him when I heard Wolfe say, "You realize, Mr. Jarrell, that there could be no commitment as to how long he would stay there. I might need him."

"Yes, certainly. I realize that."

"And the job itself, the nominal job. Isn't there a danger that it would be apparent that he isn't qualified for it?"

"No, none whatever. Not even to Miss Kent, my stenographer. No secretary I hired would know how I operate until I broke him in. But there's a detail to consider, the name. Of course his name is not as widely known as yours, but it is known. He'll have to use another name."

I had recovered enough to risk my voice. Unquestionably Wolfe had figured that, taken by surprise, I would raise a squawk, giving him an out, and equally unquestionably he was damned well going to be disappointed. I admit that after the jolt he had given me I was relieved when my voice came out perfectly okay. "About the name, Mr. Jarrell." I was talking to him, not to Wolfe. "Of course I'll have to take some luggage, quite a lot since I may be staying indefinitely, and mine has my initials on it. The usual problem. A.G. Let's see. How about Abe Goldstein?"

Jarrell, regarding me, screwed his lips. "I don't think so. No. I've got nothing against Jews, especially when they need money, but you don't look it. No."

"Well, I'll try again. I suppose you're right, I ought to look it. How about Adonis Guilfoyle?"

He laughed. It started with a cackle, then he threw his head back and roared. It tapered off to another cackle before he spoke.

11

"One thing about me, I've got a sense of humor. I could appreciate you, Goodwin, don't think I couldn't. We'll get along. You'd better let me try. A. Alan? That's all right. G. Green. Why not? Alan Green."

"Okay." I arose. "It hasn't got much flavor, but it'll do. It will take me a little while to pack, fifteen or twenty minutes." I moved.

"Archie! Sit down."

The round was mine, against big odds. He owned the house and everything in it except the furniture in my bedroom. He was the boss and paid my salary. He weighed nearly a hundred pounds more than my 178. The chair I had just got up from had cost $139.95; the one he was sitting in, oversized and custom-made of Brazilian Mauro, had come to $650.00. We were both licensed private detectives, but he was a genius and I was merely an operative. He, with or without Fritz to help, could turn out a dish of *Couronne de Canard au Riz à la Normande* without batting an eye; I had to concentrate to poach an egg. He had ten thousand orchids in his plant rooms on the roof; I had one African violet on my windowsill, and it wasn't feeling well. Etc.

But he was yelling uncle. He had counted

on getting a squawk out of me, and now he was stuck, and he would have to eat crow instead of *Couronne de Canard au Riz à la Normande* if he wanted to get unstuck.

I faced him and inquired pleasantly, "Why, don't you like Alan Green?"

"Pfui. I haven't instructed you to comply with Mr. Jarrell's suggestion."

"No, but you indicated plainly that you intended to. Very plainly."

"I intended to confer with you."

"Yes, sir. We're conferring. Points to consider: would you like to improve on Alan Green, and would it be better for me to get a thorough briefing here, and get it in my notebook, before going up there? I think maybe it would."

"Then—" He swallowed it. What had started for his tongue was probably, "Then you persist in this pigheaded perversity," or something stronger, but he knew darned well he asked for it, and there was company present. You may be thinking that the bundle of bills was also present, but I doubt if that was a factor. I have heard him turn down more than a few husbands, and more than a few wives, who had offered bigger bundles than that one if he would get them out of bliss that had gone sour. No. He knew he had lost the round, and knew that I knew it, but he wasn't going to admit it in front of a stranger.

"Very well," he said. He pushed his chair back, got up, and told Jarrell, "You will excuse me. Mr. Goodwin will know what information he needs." He circled around the red leather chair and marched out.

I sat at my desk, got notebook and pen, and swiveled to the client. "First," I said, "all the names, please."

2

I can't undertake to make you feel at home in that Fifth Avenue duplex penthouse because I never completely got the hang of it myself. By the third day I decided that two different architects had worked on it simultaneously and hadn't been on speaking terms. Jarrell had said it had twenty rooms, but I think it had seventeen or nineteen or twenty-one or twenty-three. I never made it twenty. And it wasn't duplex, it was triplex. The butler, Steck, the housekeeper, Mrs. Latham, and the two maids, Rose and Freda, slept on the floor below, which didn't count. The cook and the chauffeur slept out.

Having got it in my notebook, along with ten pages of other items, that Wyman, the son, and Lois, the daughter, were Jarrell's children by his first wife, who had died long ago, I had supposed that there were so many variations in taste among the rooms because Jarrell and the first wife and the current marital affliction, Trella, had all had a hand at it, but was set right on that the second day by Roger Foote, Trella's brother. It was decorators. At least eight decorators had been involved. Whenever Jarrell decided he didn't like the way a room looked he called in a decorator, never one he had used before, to try something else. That added to the confusion the architects had contributed. The living room, about the right size for badminton, which they called the lounge because some decorator had told them to, was blacksmith modern—black iron frames for chairs and sofas and mirrors, black iron and white tile around the fireplace, black iron and glass tables; and the dining room, on the other side of an arch, was Moorish or something. The arch itself was in a hell of a fix, a very bad case of split personality. The side terrace outside the dining room was

15

also Moorish, I guess, with mosaic tubs and boxes and table tops. It was on the first floor, which was ten stories up. The big front terrace, with access from both the reception hall and the lounge, was Du Pont frontier. The tables were redwood slabs and the chairs were chromium with webbed plastic seats. A dozen pink dogwoods in bloom, in big wooden tubs, were scattered around on Monday, the day I arrived, but when I went to the lounge at cocktail time on Wednesday they had disappeared and been replaced by rhododendrons covered with buds. I was reminded of the crack George Kaufman made once to Moss Hart—"That just shows what God could do if only he had money."

Jarrell's office, which was called the library, was also on the first floor, in the rear. When I arrived, with him, Monday afternoon, he had taken me straight there after turning my luggage over to Steck, the butler. It was a big square room with windows in only one wall, and no decorator had had a go at it. There were three desks, big, medium, and small. The big desk had four phones, red, yellow, white, and black; the medium one had three, red, white, and black; and the small one had two, white and

16

black. All of one wall was occupied by a battery of steel filing cabinets as tall as me. Another was covered by shelves to the ceiling, crammed with books and magazines; I found later that they were all strictly business, everything from *Profits in Oysters* to *North American Corporation Directory* for the past twenty years. The other wall had three doors, two big safes, a table with current magazines—also business—and a refrigerator.

Jarrell had led me across to the small desk, which was the size of mine at home, and said, "Nora, this is Alan Green, my secretary. You'll have to help me show him the ropes."

Nora Kent, seated at the desk, tilted her head back to aim a pair of gray eyes at me. Her age, forty-seven, was recorded in my notebook, but she didn't look it, even with the gray showing in her soft brown hair. But the notebook also said that she was competent, trustworthy, and nobody's fool, and she looked that. She had been with Jarrell twenty-two years. There was something about the way she offered a hand that gave me the feeling it would be more appropriate to kiss it than to grip it, but she reciprocated the clasp firmly though briefly.

17

She spoke. "Consider me at your service, Mr. Green." The gray eyes went to Jarrell. "Mr. Clay has called three times. Toledo operator seven-nineteen wants you, a Mr. William R. Bowen. From Mrs. Jarrell, there will be three guests at dinner; the names are on your desk, also a telegram. Where do you want me to start with Mr. Green?"

"There's no hurry. Let him catch his breath." Jarrell pointed to the medium-sized desk, off to the right. "That's yours, Green. Now you know your way here, and I'll be busy with Nora for a while. I told Steck— here he is." The door had opened and the butler was there. "Steck, before you show Mr. Green to his room take him around. We don't want him getting lost. Have you told Mrs. Jarrell he's here?"

"Yes, sir."

Jarrell was at his desk. "Don't come back, Green. I'll be busy. Get your bearings. Cocktails in the lounge at six-thirty."

Steck moved aside for me to pass, pulled the door shut as he backed out, said, "This way, sir," and started down the corridor a mile a minute.

I called to him, "Hold it, Steck," and he braked and turned.

"You look harassed," I told him. He did.

18

He was an inch taller than me, but thinner. His pale sad face was so long and narrow that he looked taller than he was. His black tie was a little crooked. I added, "You must have things to do."

"Yes, sir, certainly, I have duties."

"Sure. Just show me my room."

"Mr. Jarrell said to take you around, sir."

"You can do that later, if you can work it in. At the moment I need a room. I want to gargle."

"Yes, sir. This way, sir."

I followed him down the corridor and around a corner to an elevator. I asked if there were stairs and was told that there were three, one off the lounge, one in the corridor, and one for service in the rear. Also three elevators. The one we were in was gold-plated, or possibly solid. On the upper floor we went left, then right, and near the end of the hall he opened a door and bowed me in. He followed, to tell me about the phones. A ring would be for the green one, from the outside world. A buzz would be for the black one, from somewhere inside, for instance from Mr. Jarrell. I would use that one to get Steck when I was ready to be taken around. I thanked him out.

The room was twelve by sixteen, two windows with venetians, a little frilly but not bad, mostly blue and lemon-yellow except the rugs, which were tan with dark brown stripes. The bed was okay, and so was the bathroom. Under ordinary circumstances I would have used the green phone to ring Wolfe and report arrival, but I skipped it, not wanting to rub it in. After unpacking, taking my time, deciding not to shave, washing my hands, and straightening my tie, I got out my notebook, sat by a window, and turned to a list of names:

Mrs. Otis Jarrell (Trella)
Lois Jarrell, daughter by first wife
Wyman Jarrell, son by ditto
Mrs. Wyman Jarrell (Susan)
Roger Foote, Trella's brother
Nora Kent, stenographer
James L. Eber, ex-secretary
Corey Brigham, friend of family who
    queered deal

The last two didn't live there, but it seemed likely that they would need attention if I was going to get anywhere, which was doubtful. If Susan was really a snake, and if the only way to earn a fee was to get her bounced out of the house and the family, leaving her husband behind, it would take a lot of doing. My wrist watch said there was still forty minutes before cocktail time. I returned the notebook to my bag, the small one, which contained a few personal items not appropriate for Alan Green, locked the bag, left the room, found the stairs, and descended to the lower floor.

It would be inaccurate to say I got lost five times in the next quarter of an hour, since you can't get lost when you have no destination, but I certainly got confused. Neither of the architects had had any use for a straightaway, but they had had conflicting ideas on how to handle turns and corners. When I found myself passing an open door for the third time, recognizing it by the view it gave of a corner of a grand piano, and the blah of a radio or TV, with no notion of how I got there, I decided to call it off and make for the front terrace, but a voice came through to my back. "Is that you, Wy?"

I backtracked and stepped through into what, as I learned later, they called the studio.

"I'm Alan Green," I said. "Finding my way around."

She was on a couch, stretched out from the waist down, with her upper half propped against cushions. Since she was too old for either Lois or Susan, though by no means aged, she must be Trella, the marital affliction. There was a shade too much of her around the middle and above the neck—say six or eight pounds. She was a blue-eyed blonde, and her face had probably been worthy of notice before she had buried the bones too deep by thickening the stucco. What showed below the skirt hem of her blue dress—from the knees down—was still worthy of notice. While I noticed it she was reaching for a remote-control gadget, which was there beside her, to turn off the TV.

She took me in. "Secretary," she said.

"Yes, ma'am," I acknowledged. "Just hired by your husband—if you're Mrs. Otis Jarrell."

"You don't look like a secretary."

"I know, it's a handicap." I smiled at her. She invited smiles. "I try to act like one."

She put up a hand to pat a yawn—a soft little hand. "Damn it, I'm still half asleep. Television is better than a pill, don't you think so?" She patted the couch. "Come and sit down. What made you think I'm Mrs. Otis Jarrell?"

I stayed put. "To begin with, you're here. You couldn't be Miss Lois Jarrell because you must be married. You couldn't be Mrs. Wyman Jarrell because I've got the impression that my employer feels a little cool about his daughter-in-law and it seemed unlikely he would feel cool about you."

"Where did you get that impression?"

"From him. When he told me not to discuss his business affairs with anyone, including members of the family. I thought he put some emphasis on his daughter-in-law."

"Why must I be married?"

I smiled again. "You'll have to pardon me because you asked. Seeing you, and knowing what men like, I couldn't believe that you were still at large."

"Very nice." She was smiling back. "*Very* nice. My God, I don't have to pardon you for that. You don't talk like a secretary, either." She pushed the remote control gadget aside. "Sit down. Do you like leg of lamb?"

I felt that a little braking was required. It was all very well to get on a friendly basis with the mistress of the house as soon as possible, since that might be useful in trapping the snake, and the smiling and sit-downing was very nice, but her concern about feeding the new secretary right after only three minutes with him was going too far too quick. Since I didn't look like a secretary or talk like one, I thought I had better at least act like one, and I was facing up to it when help came.

There were footsteps in the corridor and a man entered. Three steps in he stopped short, at sight of me. He turned to her. "Oh. I don't need to wake you."

"Not today, Wy. This is your father's new secretary. Green. Alan Green. We were getting acquainted."

"Oh." He went to her, leaned over, and kissed her on the lips. It didn't strike me as a typical filial operation, but of course she wasn't his mother. He straightened up. "You don't look as sleepy as usual. Your eyes don't look sleepy. You've had a drink."

"No, I haven't." She was smiling at him. She gestured at me. "He woke me up. We're going to like him."

"Are we?" He turned, moved, and ex-tended a hand. "I'm Wyman Jarrell."

He was two inches shorter than me and two inches narrower across the shoulders. He had his father's brown eyes but the rest of him came from somebody else, particularly his tight little ears and thin straight nose. There were three deep creases down the middle of his brow, which at his age, twenty-seven, seemed precocious. He was going on. "I'll be talking with you, I suppose, but that's up to my father. I'll be seeing you." He turned his back on me.

I headed for the door, was told by Mrs. Jarrell there would be cocktails in the lounge at six-thirty, halted to thank her and left. As I moved down the corridor toward the front a female in uniform came around a corner and leered at me as she approached. Taken by surprise, I leered back. Evidently, I thought, this gang doesn't stand on formality. I was told later by somebody that Freda had been born with a leer, but I never went into it with Freda.

I had stepped out to the front terrace for a moment during my tour, so had already met the dogwoods and glanced around the layout of redwood slabs and chrome and plastic, and now I crossed to the parapet for a look down at Fifth Avenue and across the park. The sun was smack in my eyes, and I put a hand up to shade them for a view of a squirrel perched on a limb high in a tree, and was in that pose when a voice came from behind.

"Who are you, Sitting Bull?"

I pivoted. A girl all in white with bare tanned arms and a bare tanned throat down to the start of the curves and a tanned face with dimples and greenish brown eyes and a pony tail was coming. If you are thinking that is too much to take in with a quick glance, I am a detective and a trained observer. I had time not only to take her in but also to think, Good Lord, if that's Susan and she's a snake I'm going to take up herpetology, if that's the word, and I can look it up.

She was still five steps off when I spoke. "Me good Indian. Me good friend white men, only you're not a man and you're not white. I was looking at a squirrel. My name is Alan Green. I am the new secretary, hired today. I was told to get my bearings and have been trying to. I have met your husband."

"Not *my* husband, you haven't. I'm a spinster named Lois. Do you like squirrels?"

"It depends. A squirrel with integrity and charm, with no bad habits, a squirrel who votes right, who can be counted on in a pinch, I like *that* squirrel." At close quarters they weren't what I would call dimples, just little cheek dips that caught shadows if the light angle was right. "I hope I don't sound fussy."

"Come here a minute." She led me off to the right, put a hand on the tiled top of the parapet, and with the other pointed across the avenue. "See that tree? See the one I mean?"

"The one that lost an arm."

"That's it. One day in March a squirrel was skipping around on it, up near the top. I was nine years old. My father had given my brother a rifle for his birthday. I went and got the rifle and loaded it, and came out and stood here, right at this spot, and waited until the squirrel stopped to rest, and shot it. It tumbled off. On the way down it bumped against limbs twice. I yelled for Wy, my brother, and he came and I showed it to him, there on the ground not moving, and he—but the rest doesn't matter. With anyone I might possibly fall in love with I like to start off by telling him the worst thing I ever did, and anyway you brought it up by saying you were looking at a squirrel. Now you know the worst, unless you think it's worse that several years later I wrote a

27

poem called 'Requiem for a Rodent.' It was published in my school paper."

"Certainly it's worse. Running it down by calling it a rodent, even though it was one."

She nodded. "I've suspected it myself. Some day I'll get analyzed and find out." She waved it away, into the future. "Where did you ever get the idea of being a secretary?"

"In a dream. Years ago. In the dream I was the secretary of a wealthy pirate. His beautiful daughter was standing on the edge of a cliff shooting at a gopher, which is a rodent, down on the prairie, and when she hit it she felt so sorry for it that she jumped off the cliff. I was down below and caught her, saving her life, and it ended romantically. So I became a secretary."

Her brows were lifted, opening her eyes as wide as they would go. "I can't imagine how a pirate's daughter happened to be standing on a cliff on top of a prairie. You must have been dreaming."

No man could stop a conversation as dead in its tracks as that. It takes a woman. But at least she had the decency to start up another one. With her eyes back to normal, she cocked her head a little to the side and said, "You know, I'm bothered. I'm sure

I've seen you before somewhere and I can't remember where, and I always remember people. Where was it? Have you forgotten too?"

I had known that might come from one or more of them. My picture hadn't been in the papers as often as the president of Egypt's, or even Nero Wolfe's, and the latest had been nearly a year ago, but I had known it might happen. I grinned at her. I hadn't been grinning in any published picture. One thing, it gave me a chance to recover the ball she had taken away from me.

I shook my head. "I wouldn't forget. I only forget faces I don't care to remember. The only way I can account for it, you must have seen me in a dream."

She laughed. "All right, now we're even. I wish I could remember. Of course I may have seen you in a theater or restaurant, but if that's it and I do remember I won't tell you, because it would puff you up. Only you'll need puffing up after you've been here a while. He's my dear father, but he must be terrible to work for. I don't see— Hi, Roger. Have you met Alan Green? Dad's new secretary. Roger Foote."

I had turned. Trella's brother bore as

little resemblance to her as Wyman Jarrell had to his father. He was big and broad and brawny, with no stuffing at all between the skin and bones of his big wide face. If his size and setup hadn't warned me I might have got some knuckles crushed by his big paw; as it was, I gave as good as I got and it was a draw.

"Muscle man," he said. "My congratulations. Trust the filly to arch her neck at you. Ten to one she told you about the squirrel."

"Roger," Lois told me, "is horsy. He nearly went to the Kentucky Derby. He even owned a horse once, but it sprang a leak. No Pimlico today, Roger?"

"No, my angel. I could have got there, but I might never have got back. Your father has told Western Union not to deliver collect telegrams from me. Not to mention collect phone calls." He switched to me. "Do you suppose you're going to stick it?"

"I couldn't say, Mr. Foote. I've only been here two hours. Why, is it rough going?"

"It's worse than rough. Even if you're not a panhandler like me. My brother-in-law is made of iron. They could have used him to make that godawful stuff in the lounge, and I wish they had. Look at the Derby. I was on Iron Liege, or would have been if I had had it. I could have made myself independent for a week or more. You get the connection. You would think a man made of iron would stake me for a go on Iron Liege? No." He lifted a hand to look at it, saw it was empty, and dropped it. "I must have left my drink inside. You're not thirsty?"

"I am," Lois declared. "You, Mr. Green? Or Alan. We make free with the secretary." She moved. "Come along."

I followed them into the lounge, and across to a portable bar where Otis Jarrell, with a stranger at each elbow, a man and a woman, was stirring a pitcher of Martinis. The man was a wiry little specimen, black-eyed and black-haired, very neat in charcoal, with a jacket that flared at the waist. The woman, half a head taller, had red hair that was either natural or not, a milk-white face, and a jaw. Jarrell introduced me, but I didn't get their names until later: Mr. and Mrs. Herman Dietz. They weren't interested in the new secretary. Roger Foote moved to the other side of the bar and produced a Bloody Mary for Lois, a scotch and water for me, and a double bourbon with no accessories for himself.

I took a healthy sip and looked around.

Wyman, the son, and Nora Kent, the stenographer, were standing over near the fireplace, which had no fire, presumably talking business. Not far off Trella was relaxed in a big soft chair, looking up at a man who was perched on one of the arms.

Lois' voice came up to my ear. "You've met my stepmother, haven't you?"

I told her yes, but not the man, and she said he was Corey Brigham, and was going to add something but decided not to. I was surprised to see him there, since he was on my list as the guy who had spoiled a deal, but the guests had been invited by her, not him. Or maybe not. Possibly Jarrell had suggested it, counting on bringing me home with him and wanting me to meet him. From a distance he was no special treat. Leaning over Trella with a well-trained smile, he had all the earmarks of a middle-aged million-dollar smoothie who would slip a head waiter twenty bucks and tip a hackie a dime. I was taking him in, filing him under unfinished business, when he lifted his head and turned it left, and I turned mine to see what had got his attention.

The snake had entered the room.

3

OF course it could have been that she planned it that way, that she waited until everyone else was there to make her entrance, and then, floating in, deliberately underplayed it. But also it could have been that she didn't like crowds, even family crowds, and put it off as long as she could, and then having to go through with it, made herself as small and quiet as possible. I reserved my opinion, without prejudice—or rather, with two prejudices striking a balance. The attraction of the snake theory was that she had to be one if we were going to fill our client's order. The counterattraction was that I didn't like the client and wouldn't have minded seeing him stub his toe. So my mind was open as I watched her move across toward the fireplace, to where her husband was talking with Nora Kent. There was nothing reptilian about the way she moved. It might be said that she glided, but she didn't slither. She was slender, not tall, with a small oval face. Her husband kissed her on the cheek, then headed for the bar, presumably to get her a drink.

Trella called my name, Alan, making free with the secretary, and I went over to her and was introduced to Corey Brigham. When she patted the vacant arm of the chair and told me to sit I did so, thinking it safer there than it had been in the studio, and Brigham got up and left. She said I hadn't answered her question about leg of lamb, and she wanted to know. It seemed possible that I had got her wrong, that her idea was merely to function as a helpmate and see to it that the hired help liked the grub—but no. She might have asked it, but she didn't; she cooed it. I may not know as much about women as Wolfe pretends he thinks I do, but I know a coo when I hear it.

While giving her due attention as my hostess and my boss's wife, I was observing a phenomenon from the corner of my eye. When Wyman returned to Susan with her drink, Roger Foote was there. Also Corey Brigham was wandering over to them, and in a couple of minutes there went Herman Dietz. So four of the six males present were gathered around Susan, but as far as I could see she hadn't bent a finger or slanted an eye to get them there. Jarrell was still at the bar with Dietz's redheaded wife. Lois and Nora Kent had stepped out to the terrace.

Apparently Trella had seen what the corner of my eye was doing, for she said, "You have to be closer to appreciate her. She blurs at a distance."

"Her? Who?"

She patted my arm. "Now now. I don't mind, I'm used to it. Susan. My step-daughter-in-law. Go and put an oar in."

"She seems to have a full crew. Anyway, I haven't met her."

"You haven't? That won't do." She turned and sang out, "Susan! Come here."

She was obeyed instantly. The circle opened to make room, and Susan crossed to us. "Yes, Trella?"

"I want to present Mr. Green. Alan. He has taken Jim's place. He has met everyone but you, and that didn't seem fair."

I took the offered hand and felt it warm and firm for the fifth of a second she let me have it. Her face *had* blurred at a distance. Even close up none of her features took your eye; you only saw the whole, the little oval face.

"Welcome to our aerie, Mr. Green," she said. Her voice was low, and was shy or coy or wary or demure, depending on your attitude. I had no attitude, and didn't intend to have one until I could give reasons. All I would have conceded on the spot was that she didn't hiss like a cobra or rattle like a rattler. As for her being the only one of the bunch to bid me welcome, that was sociable and kindhearted, but it would seem that she might have left that to the lady of the house. I thanked her for it anyway. She glanced at Trella, apparently uncertain whether to let it go at that or stay for a chat, murmured something polite, and moved away.

"I think it's in her bones," Trella said. "Or maybe her blood. Anyhow it's nothing you can see or hear. Some kind of hypnotism, but I think she can turn it on and off. Did you feel anything?"

"I'm a secretary, Mrs. Jarrell. Secretaries don't feel."

"The hell they don't. Jim Eber did. Of course you've barely met her and you may be immune."

Trella was telling me about a book on hypnotism she had read when Steck came to tell her dinner was ready.

It was uneven, five women and six men, and I was put between Lois and Roger Foote. There were several features deserving comment. The stenographer not only ate with the family, she sat next to Jarrell. The housekeeper, Mrs. Latham, helped serve. I had always thought a housekeeper was above it. Roger Foote, who had had enough to drink, ate like a truck driver—no, cut that—like a panhandler. The talk was spotty, mostly neighbor-to-neighbor, except when Corey Brigham sounded off about the Eisenhower budget. The leg of lamb was first-rate, not up to Fritz's but good. I noticed Trella noticing me the second time around. The salad was soggy. I'm not an expert on wine, but I doubted if it deserved the remarks it got from Herman Dietz.

As we were passing through the Moorish arch—half-Moorish, anyway—to return to the lounge for coffee, Trella asked me if I played bridge, and Jarrell heard her.

"Not tonight," he said. "I need him. I won't be here tomorrow. You've got enough."

"Not without Nora. You know Susan doesn't play."

"I don't need Nora. You can have her."

If Susan had played, and if I could have swung it to be at her table, I would have been sorry to miss it. Perhaps you don't know all there is to know about a woman after watching her at an evening of bridge, but you should know more than when you sat down. By the time we were through with coffee they had chosen partners and Steck had the tables ready. I had wondered if Susan would go off to her pit, but apparently not. When Jarrell and I left she was out on the terrace.

He led the way through the reception hall, across a Kirman twice as big as my room at home—I have a Kirman there, paid for by me, 8′4″ x 3′2″—down the corridor, and around a couple of corners, to the door of the library. Taking a key fold from a pocket, he selected one, used it, and pushed the door open; and light came at us, sudden and so strong it made me blink. I may also have jumped.

He laughed, closing the key fold. "That's my idea." He pointed above the door. "See the clock? Anyone coming in, his picture is taken, and the clock shows the time. Not only that, it goes by closed circuit to the Horland Protective Agency, only three blocks away. A man there saw us come in just now. There's a switch at my desk and when we're in here we turn it off—Nora or I. I've got them at the doors of the apartment too, front and back. By the way, I'll give you keys. With this I don't have to wonder about keys—for instance, Jim Eber could have had duplicates made. I don't give a damn if he did. What do you think of it?"

"Very neat. Expensive, but neat. I ought to mention, if someone at Horland's saw me come in with you, he may know me, by sight anyway. A lot of them do. Does that matter?"

"I doubt it." He had turned on lights and gone to his desk. "I'll call them. Damn it, I could have come in first and switched it off. I'll call them. Sit down. Have a cigar?"

It was the cigar he had lit in the lounge after dinner that had warned me to keep my eyes on the road. I don't smoke them my-self, but I admit that the finest tobacco smell you can get is a whiff from the lit end of a fine Havana, and when the box had been passed I had noticed that they were Portanagas. But I had not enjoyed the whiff I had got from the one Jarrell had lit. In fact, I had snorted it out. That was bad. When you can't stand the smell of a Portanaga because a client is smoking it, watch out or you'll be giving him the short end of the stick, which is unethical. Any-way, I saved him three bucks by not taking one.

He leaned back, let smoke float out of his mouth, and inquired, "What impression did you get?"

I looked judicious. "Not much of any. I only spoke a few words with her. Your suggestion that I get the others talking about her, especially your wife and your wife's brother—there has been no opportunity for that, and there won't be while they're playing cards. I think I ought to cultivate Corey Brigham."

He nodded. "You saw how it was there before dinner."

"Sure. Also Foote and Dietz, not to mention your son. Your wife thinks she hypnotizes them."

"You don't know what my wife thinks. You only know what she says she thinks. Then you discussed her with my wife?"

"Not at any length. I don't quite see when I'm going to discuss her at length with any of them. I don't see how this is going to work. As your secretary I should be spending my day in here with you and Miss Kent, and if they spend their evening at bridge?"

"I know." He tapped ash off in a tray. "You won't have to spend tomorrow in here. I'm taking a morning plane to Toledo, and I don't know when I'll be back. Actually my secretary had damn little to do when I'm not here. Nora knows everything, and I'll tell her to forget about you until I return. As I told you this afternoon, I'm certain that everybody here, every damn one of them, knows things about my daughter-in-law that I don't know. Even my daughter. Even Nora." His eyes were leveled at me. "It's up to you. I've told you about my wife, she'll talk your head off, but anything she tells you may or may not be so. Do you dance?"

"Yes."

"Are you a good dancer?"

"Yes."

"Lois likes to dance, but she's particular. Take her out tomorrow evening. Has Roger hit you for a loan yet?"

"No. I haven't been alone with him."

"That wouldn't stop him. When he does, let him have fifty or a hundred. Give him the impression that you stand in well with me—even let him think you have something on me. Buy my wife some flowers—nothing elaborate, as long as it's something she thinks you paid for. She loves to have men buy things for her. You might take her to lunch, to Rusterman's, and tip high. When a man tips high she takes it as a personal compliment."

I wanted to move my chair back a little to get less of his cigar, but vetoed it. "I don't object to the program personally," I said, "but I do professionally. That's a hell of a schedule for a secretary. They're not halfwits."

"That doesn't matter." He flipped it off with the cigar. "Let them all think you have something on me—let them think anything they want to. The point is that the house is mine and the money is mine, and whatever I stand for they'll accept whether they understand it or not. The only exception to that is my daughter-in-law, and that's what you're here for. She's making a horse's ass out of my son, and she's getting him away from me, and she's sticking a finger in my affairs. I'm making you a proposition. The day she's out of here, with my son staying, you get ten thousand dollars in cash, in addition to any fee Nero Wolfe charges. The day a divorce settles it, with my son still staying, you get fifty thousand. You personally. That will be in addition to any expenses you incur, over and above Wolfe's fee and expenses."

I said that no man can stop a conversation

the way a woman can, but I must admit that Otis Jarrell had made a darned good stab at it. I also admit I was flattered. Obviously he had gone to Wolfe just to get me, to get me there in his library so he could offer me sixty grand and expenses to frame his daughter-in-law, who probably wasn't a snake at all. If she had been, his itch to get rid of her would have been legitimate, and he could have left it as a job for Wolfe and just let me earn my salary.

It sure was flattering. "That's quite a proposition," I said, "but there's a hitch. I work for Mr. Wolfe. He pays me."

"You'll still be working for him. I only want you to do what I hired him to do. He'll get his fee."

That was an insult to my intelligence. He didn't have to make it so damned plain. It would have been a pleasure to square my shoulders and lift my chin and tell him to take back his gold and go climb a tree, and that would have been the simplest way out, but there were drawbacks. For one thing, it was barely possible that she really was a snake and no framing would be required. For another, if she wasn't a snake, and if he was determined to frame her, she needed to know it and deserved to know it, but he was still Wolfe's client, and all I had was what he had said to me with no witness present. For still another, there was the ten grand in Wolfe's safe, not mine to spurn. For one more if we need it, I have my full share of curiosity.

I tightened my face to look uncomfortable. "I guess," I said, "I'll have to tell Mr. Wolfe about your proposition. I think I will. I've got to protect myself."

"Against what?" he demanded.

"Well . . . for instance, you might talk in your sleep."

He laughed. "I like you, Goodwin. I knew we'd get along. This is just you and me, and you don't need protection any more than I do. You know your way around and so do I. What do you want now for expenses? Five thousand? Ten?"

"Nothing. Let it ride and we'll see." I loosened the face. "I'm not accepting your proposition, Mr. Jarrell. I'm not even considering it. If I ever found myself feeling like accepting it, I'd meet you somewhere that I was sure wasn't wired for sound. After all, Horland's Protective Agency might be listening right now."

He laughed again. "You *are* cagey."

"Not cagey, I just don't want my hair

44

mussed. Do you want me to go on with the program? As you suggested?"

"Certainly I do. I think we understand each other, Goodwin." He put a fist on the desk. "I'll tell you this, since you probably know it anyway. I'd give a million dollars cash any minute to get rid of that woman for good and call it a bargain. That doesn't mean you can play me for a sucker. I'll pay for what I get, but not for what I don't get. Any arrangements you make, I want to know who with and for exactly what and how much."

"You will. Have you any more suggestions?"

He didn't have, at least nothing specific. Even after proposing, as it looked to me, an out-and-out frame, he still thought, or pretended to, that I might raise some dust by cultivating the inmates. He tried to insist on an advance of expenses, but I said no, I would ask for it if and when needed. I was surprised that he didn't refer again to my notion that I might have to tell Wolfe about his proposition; apparently he was taking it for granted that I would take my bread buttered on both sides if the butter was thick enough. He was sure we understood each other, but I wasn't. I wasn't sure of anything. Before I went he gave me two keys, one for the front door and one for the library. He said he had to make a phone call, and I said I was going out for a walk. He said I could use the phone there, or in my room, and I said that wasn't it, I always took a little walk in the evening. Maybe we understood each other at that, up to a point.

I went to the front vestibule, took the private elevator down, nodded at the sentinel in the lobby—not the one who had been there when I arrived—walked east to Madison, found a phone booth, and dialed a number.

After one buzz a voice was in my ear. "Nero Wolfe's residence, Orville Cather speaking."

I was stunned. It took me a full second to recover. Then I spoke, through my nose. "This is the city mortuary. We have a body down here, a young man with classic Grecian features who jumped off Brooklyn Bridge. Papers in his wallet identify him as Archie Goodwin and his address—"

"Toss it back in the river," Orrie said. "What good is it? It never was much good anyway."

"Okay," I said, not through my nose.

"Now I know. May I please speak to Mr. Wolfe?"

"I'll see. He's reading a book. Hold it."

I did so, and in a moment got a growl. "Yes?"

"I went for a walk, and am in a booth. Reporting: the bed is good and the food is edible. I have met the family and they are not mine, except possibly the daughter, Lois. She shot a squirrel and wrote a poem about it. I'm glad you've got Orrie to answer the phone and do the chores because that may simplify matters. You can stop my salary as of now. Jarrell has offered me sixty grand and expenses, me personally, to get the goods on his daughter-in-law and bounce her. I think the idea is that the goods are to be handmade, by me, but he didn't say so in so many words. If it takes me twelve weeks that will be five grand a week, so my salary would be peanuts and you can forget it. I'll get it in cash, no tax to pay, and then I'll probably marry Lois. Oh yes, you'll get your fee too."

"How much of this is flummery?"

"None of the facts. The facts are straight. I am reporting."

"Then he's either a nincompoop or a scalawag or both."

"Probably but not necessarily. He said he would give a million dollars to get rid of her and consider it a bargain. So it's just possible he has merely got an itch he can't scratch and is temporarily nuts. I'm giving him the benefit of the doubt because he's your client."

"And yours."

"No, sir. I didn't accept. I declined an advance for expenses. I turned him down, but with a manner and a tone of voice that sort of left it hanging. He thinks I'm just being cagey. What I think, I think he expects me to fix up a stew that will boil her alive, but I have been known to think wrong. I admit it's conceivable that she has it coming to her. One thing, she attracts men without apparently trying to. If a woman gathers them around by working a come-on, that's okay, they have a choice, they can play or not as they please. But when they come just because she's there, with no invitation visible to the naked eye, and I have good eyes, look out. She may not be a snake, in fact she may be an angel, but angels can be more dangerous than snakes and usually are. I can stick around and try to tag her, or you can return the ten grand and cross it off. Which?"

He grunted. "Mr. Jarrell has taken me for a donkey."

"And me for a goop. Our pride is hurt. He ought to pay for the privilege, one way or another. I'll keep you informed of developments, if any."

"Very well."

"Please remind Orrie that the bottom drawer of my desk is personal and there's nothing in it he needs."

He said he would, and even said good night before he hung up. I bought a picture postcard at the rack, and a stamp, addressed the card to Fritz, and wrote on it, "Having wonderful time. Wish you were here. Archie," went and found a mailbox and dropped the card in, and returned to the barracks.

In the tenth-floor vestibule I gave my key a try, found that it worked, and was dazzled by no flash of light as I entered, so the thing hadn't been turned on for the night. As I crossed the reception hall I was thinking that the security setup wasn't as foolproof as Jarrell thought, until I saw that Speck had appeared around a corner for a look at me. He certainly had his duties.

I went to him and spoke. "Mr. Jarrell gave me a key."

"Yes, sir."

"Is he around?"

"In the library, sir, I think."

"They're playing cards?"

"Yes, sir."

"If you're not tied up I cordially invite you to my room for some gin. I mean gin rummy."

He batted an eye. "Thank you, sir, but I have my duties."

"Some other time. Is Mrs. Wyman Jarrell on the terrace?"

"I think not, sir. I think she's in the studio."

"Is that on this floor?"

"Yes, sir. The main corridor, on the right. Where you were with Mrs. Jarrell this afternoon."

Now how the hell did he know that? Also, was it proper for a butler to let me know he knew it? I suspected not. I suspected that my gin invitation, if it hadn't actually crashed the sound barrier, had made a dent in it. I headed for the corridor and for the rear, and will claim no credit for spotting the door because it was standing open and voices were emerging. Entering, I was in semi-darkness. The only light came from the corridor and the television screen, which showed the emcee and the panel members of "Show Your Slip." The voices were theirs. Turning, I saw her, dimly, in a chair.

"Do you mind if I join you?" I asked.

"Of course not," she said, barely loud enough. That was all she said. I moved to a chair to her left, and sat.

I have no TV favorites, because most of the programs seem to be intended for either the under-brained or the over-brained and I come in between, but if I had, "Show Your Slip" wouldn't be one of them. If it's one of yours, you can assume you have more brains than I have, and what I assume is my own affair. I admit I didn't give it my full attention that evening because I was conscious of Susan there within arm's reach, and was keeping myself receptive for any sinister influences that might be oozing from her, or angelic ones either. I felt none. All that got to me was a faint trace of a perfume that reminded me of the one Lily Rowan uses, but it wasn't quite the same.

When the windup commercial started she reached to the chair on her other side, to the control, and the sound stopped and the picture went. That made it still darker. The pale blur of her face turned to me. "What channel do you want, Mr. Green?"

"None particularly. Mr. Jarrell finished with me, and the others were playing cards, and I heard it going and came in. Whatever you want."

"I was just passing the time. There's nothing I care for at ten-thirty."

"Then let's skip it. Do you mind if we have a little light?"

"Of course not."

I went to the wall switch at the door, flipped it, and returned to the chair, and her little oval face was no longer a pale blur. I had the impression that she was trying to produce a smile for me and couldn't quite make it.

"I don't want to intrude," I said. "If I'm in the way—"

"Not at all." Her low voice, shy or coy or wary or demure, made you feel that there should be more of it, and that when there was you would like to be present to hear it. "Since you'll be living here it will be nice to get acquainted with you. I was wondering what you are like, and now you can tell me."

"I doubt it. I've been wondering about it myself and can't decide."

The smile got through. "So to begin with, you're witty. What else? Do you go to church?"

"No. Should I?"

"I don't know because I don't know you yet. I don't go as often as I should. I noticed you didn't eat any salad at dinner. Don't you like salad?"

"Yes."

"Aha!" A tiny flash came and went in her eyes. "So you're frank too. You didn't like *that* salad. I have been wanting to speak to my mother-in-law about it, but I haven't dared. I think I'm doing pretty well. You're witty, and you're frank. What do you think about when you're alone with nothing to do?"

"Let's see. I've got to make it both frank and witty. I think about the best and quickest way to do what I would be doing if I were doing something."

She nodded. "A silly question deserves a silly answer. I guess it was witty too, so that's all right. I would love to be witty—you know, to sparkle. Do you suppose you could teach me how?"

"Now look," I protested, "how could I answer that? It makes three assumptions—that I'm witty, that you're not, and that you have something to learn from me. That's more than I can handle. Try one with only one assumption."

"I'm sorry," she said. "I didn't realize. But I do think you could teach me— Oh!" She looked at her wrist watch. "I forgot!" She got up—floated up—and was looking down at me. "I must make a phone call. I'm sorry if I annoyed you, Mr. Green. Next time, you ask questions." She glided to the door and was gone.

I'll tell you exactly how it was. I wasn't aware that I had moved until I found myself halfway to the door and taking another step. Then I stopped, and told myself, I will be damned, you might think she had me on a chain. I looked back at the chair I had left; I had covered a good ten feet before I had realized I was being pulled.

I went and stood in the doorway and considered the situation. I started with a basic fact: she was a little female squirt. Okay. She hadn't fed me a potion. She hadn't stuck a needle in me. She hadn't used any magic words, far from it. She hadn't touched me. But I had come to that room with the idea of opening her up for inspection, and had ended by springing up automatically to follow her out of the room like a lapdog, and the worst of it was I didn't know why. I am perfectly willing to be attracted by a woman and to enjoy the consequences, but I want to know what's going on. I am not willing to be pulled by a string without seeing the string. Not only that; my interest in this particular specimen was supposed to be strictly professional.

I had an impulse to go to the library and tell Jarrell he was absolutely right, she was a snake. I had another impulse to go find her and tell her something. I didn't know what, but tell her. I had another one, to pack up and go home and tell Wolfe we were up against a witch and what we needed was a stake to burn her at. None of them seemed to be what the situation called for, so I found the stairs and went up to bed.

—4—

By Wednesday night, forty-eight hours later, various things had happened, but if I had made any progress I didn't know it.

Tuesday I took Trella to lunch at Rusterman's. That was a little sticky, since I was well known there, but I phoned Felix that I was working on a case incognito and told him to pass the word that I mustn't be recognized. When we arrived, though, I was sorry I hadn't picked another restaurant. Evidently everybody, from the doorman on up to Felix, knew Mrs. Jarrell too, and I couldn't blame them for being curious when, working on a case incognito, I turned up with an old and valued customer. They handled it pretty well, except when Bruno brought my check he put a pencil down beside it. A waiter supplies a pencil only when he knows the check is going to be signed and that your credit is good. I ignored it, hoping that Trella was ignoring it too, and when Bruno brought the change from my twenty I waved it away, hoping he wouldn't think I was setting a precedent.

She had said one thing that I thought worth filing. I had brought Susan's name into the conversation by saying that perhaps I should apologize for being indiscreet the day before, when I mentioned the impression I had got that Jarrell felt cool about his daughter-in-law, and she said that if I wanted to apologize, all right, but not for being indiscreet, for being wrong. She said her husband wasn't cool about Susan, he was hot. I said okay, then I would switch from cool to hot and apologize for that. Hot about what?

"What do you think?" Her blue eyes widened. "About her. She slapped him. Oh, for God's sake, quit trying to look innocent! Your first day as his secretary, and spending the morning on the terrace with Lois and taking me to Rusterman's for lunch! Secretary!"

"But he's away. He said to mark time."

"He'll get a report from Nora when he comes back, and you know it. I'm not a fool, Alan, really I'm not. I might be fairly bright if I wasn't so damn lazy. You probably know more about my husband than I do. So quit looking innocent."

"I have to look innocent, I'm his secretary. So does Steck, he's his butler. As for what I know, I didn't know Susan had slapped him. Were you there?"

"Nobody was there. I don't mean slapped him with her hand, she wouldn't do that. I don't know how she did it, probably just by looking at him. She can look a man on or look him off, either way. I wouldn't have thought any woman could look *him* off, I'd think she'd need a hatpin or a red-hot poker, but that was before I had met her. Before she moved in. Has she given you a sign yet?"

"No." I didn't know whether I was lying or not. "I'm not sure I'm up with you. If I am, I'm innocent enough to be shocked. Susan is his son's wife."

"Well. What of it?"

"It seems a little undignified. He's not an ape."

She reached to pat the back of my hand. "I must have been wrong about you. Look innocent all you want to. Certainly he's an ape. Everybody knows that. Since I'm in walking distance I might as well do a little shopping. Would you care to come along?"

I declined with thanks.

On my way uptown, walking the thirty blocks to stretch my legs, I had to decide whether to give Wolfe a ring or not. If I did, and reported the development, that Trella said our client had made a pass at his daughter-in-law and had been looked off, and that therefore it seemed possible he had hired Wolfe and tried to suborn me only to cure an acute case of pique, I would certainly be instructed to pack and come home; and I preferred to hang on a while, at least long enough to expose myself to Susan once more and see how it affected my pulse and respiration. And if I rang Wolfe and didn't report the development, I had nothing to say, so I saved a dime.

Mrs. Wyman Jarrell was out, Steck said, and so was Miss Jarrell. He also said that Mr. Foote had asked to be informed when I returned, and I said all right, inform him. Thinking it proper to make an appearance at my desk before nightfall, I left my hat and topcoat in the closet around the corner and went to the library. Nora Kent was at Jarrell's desk, using the red phone, and I moseyed over to the battery of filing cabinets and pulled out a drawer at random. The first folder was marked PAPER PRODUCTION BRAZIL, and I took it out for a look.

I was fingering through it when Nora's voice came at my back. "Did you want something, Mr. Green?"

I turned. "Nothing special. It would be nice to do something useful. If the secretary should be acquainted with these files I think I could manage it in two or three years."

"Oh, it won't take you that long. When Mr. Jarrell gets back he'll get you started."

"That's polite, and I appreciate it. You might have just told me to keep hands off." I replaced the folder and closed the drawer.

59

"Can I help with anything? Like emptying a wastebasket or changing a desk blotter?"

"No, thank you. It would be a little presumptuous of me to tell you to keep hands off since Mr. Jarrell has given you a key."

"So it would. I take it back. Have you heard from him?"

"Yes, he phoned about an hour ago. He'll return tomorrow, probably soon after noon."

There was something about her, her tone and manner, that wasn't just right. Not that it didn't fit a stenographer speaking to a secretary; of course, I had caught on that calling her a stenographer was like calling Willie Mays a bat boy. I can't very well tell you what it was, since I didn't know. I only felt that there was something between her and me, one-way, that I wasn't on to. I was thinking a little more conversation might give me an idea, when a phone buzzed.

She lifted the receiver of the black one, spoke and listened briefly, and turned to me. "For you. Mr. Foote."

I went and took it. "Hello, Roger?" I call panhandlers by their first names. "Alan."

"You're a hell of a secretary. Where have you been all day?"

"Out and around. I'm here now."

"So I hear. I understand you're a gin

60

player. Would you care to win a roll? Since Old Ironsides is away and you're not needed."

"Sure, why not? Where?"

"My room. Come on up. From your room turn right, first left, and I'll be at my door."

"Right." I hung up, told Nora I would be glad to run an errand if she had one, was assured that she hadn't, and left. So, I thought, Roger was on pumping terms with the butler. It was unlikely that Steck had volunteered the information that I had invited him to a friendly game.

Foote's room was somewhat larger than mine, with three windows, and it was all his. The chairs were green leather, and the size and shape of one of them, over by a window, would have been approved even by Wolfe. Fastened to the walls with Scotch Tape were pictures of horses, mostly in color, scores of them, all sizes. The biggest one was Native Dancer, from the side, with his head turned to see the camera.

"Not one," Roger said, "that hasn't carried my money. Muscle. Beautiful! When I open my eyes in the morning there they are. Something to wake up to. That's all any man can expect, something to wake up to. You agree?"

I did.

I had supposed, naturally, that the idea would be something like a quarter a point, maybe more, and that if he won I would pay, and if I won he would owe me. But no, it was purely social, a cent a point. Either he gambled only on the beautiful muscles, or he was stringing me along, or he merely wanted to establish relations for future use. He was a damn good gin player. He could talk about anything and did, and at the same time remember every discard and every pickup. I won 92 cents, but only because I got most of the breaks.

At one point I took advantage of something he had said. "That reminds me," I told him, "of a remark I overheard today. What do you think of a man who makes a pass at his son's wife?"

He was dealing. His hand stopped for an instant and then flipped me a card. "Who made the remark?"

"I'd rather not say. I wasn't eavesdropping, but I happened to hear it."

"Any name's mentioned?"

"Certainly."

He picked up his hand. "Your name's Alfred?"

"Alan."

"I forget names. People's. Not horses'. I'll tell you, Alan. For what I think about my brother-in-law's attitude on money and his wife's brother, come to me any time. Beyond that I'm no authority. Anyone who thinks he ought to be shot, they can shoot him. No flowers. Not from me. Your play."

That didn't tell me much. When, at six o'clock, I said I had to wash and change for a date with Lois, and he totaled the score, fast and accurate, he turned it around for me to check. "At the moment," he said, "I haven't got ninety-two cents, but you can make it ninety-two dollars. More. Peach Fuzz in the fifth at Jamaica Thursday will be eight to one. With sixty dollars I could put forty on his nose. Three hundred and twenty, and half to you. And ninety-two cents."

I told him it sounded very attractive and I'd let him know tomorrow. Since Jarrell had said to let him have fifty or a hundred I could have dished it out then and there, but if I did he probably wouldn't be around tomorrow, and there was an off chance that I would want him for something. He took it like a gentleman, no shoving.

When, that morning on the terrace, I had proposed dinner and dance to Lois, I had mentioned the Flamingo Club, but the experience at Rusterman's with Trella had shown me it wouldn't be advisable. So I asked her if she would mind making it Colonna's in the Village, where there was a good band and no one knew me, at least not by name, and we weren't apt to run into any of my friends. For a second she did mind, but then decided it would be fun to try one she had never been to.

Jarrell had said she was particular about her dancing partners, and she had a right to be. The rhythm was clear through her, not just from her hips down, and she was right with me in everything we tried. To give her as good as she gave I had to put the mind away entirely and let the body take over, and the result was that when midnight came, and time for champagne, I hadn't made a single stab at the project I was supposed to be working on. As the waiter was pouring I was thinking. What the hell, a detective has to get the subject feeling intimate before he can expect her to discuss intimate matters, and three more numbers ought to do it. Actually I never did get it started. It just happened that when we returned to the table again and finished the champagne, she lifted her glass with the last thimbleful, said,

"To life and death," and tossed it down. She put the glass on the table and added, "If death ever slept."

"I'm with you," I said, putting my empty glass next to hers, "or I guess I am. What does it mean?"

"I don't know. I ought to, since I wrote it myself. It's from that poem I wrote. The last five lines go:

"Or a rodent kept
   High and free on the twig of a tree,
Or a girl who wept
   A bitter tear for the death so near,
If death ever slept!"

"I'm sorry," I said. "I like the sound of it, but I'm still not sure what it means."

"Neither am I. That's why I'm sure it's a poem. Susan understands it, or says she does. She says there's one thing wrong with it, that instead of 'a bitter tear' it ought to be 'a welcome tear.' I don't like it. Do you?"

"I like 'bitter' better. Is Susan strong on poems?"

"I don't really know. I don't understand her any better than I understand that poem. I think she's strong on Susan, but of course

65

she's my sister-in-law and her bedroom is bigger than mine, and I'm afraid of my brother when I'm not fighting with him, so I probably hate her. I'll find out when I get analyzed."

I nodded. "That'll do it. I noticed last evening the males all gathered around except your father. Apparently he didn't even see her."

"He saw her all right. If he doesn't see a woman it's because she's not there. Do you know what a satyr is?"

"More or less."

"Look it up in the dictionary. I did once. I don't believe my father is a satyr because half the time his mind is on something else—making more money. He's just a tomcat. What's that they're starting? 'Mocajuba?' "

It was. I got up and and circled the table to pull her chair back.

To be fair to Wednesday, it's true that it was more productive than Tuesday, but that's not saying I got any farther along. It added one more to my circle of acquaintances. That was in the morning, just before noon. Having turned in around two and stayed in bed for my preferred minimum of eight hours, as I went downstairs I was thinking that breakfast would probably be a problem, but headed for the dining room anyway just to see, and in half a minute there was Steck with orange juice. I said that and coffee would hold me until lunch, but no, sir. In ten minutes he brought toast and bacon and three poached eggs and two kinds of jam and a pot of coffee. That attended to, in company with the morning *Times*, I went to the library and spent half an hour not chatting with Nora Kent. She was there, and I was willing to converse, but she either had things to do or made things to do, so after a while I gave up and departed. She did say that Jarrell's plane would be due at La Guardia at 3:05 p.m.

Strolling along the corridor toward the front and seeing that my watch said 11:56, I thought I might as well stop in at the studio for the twelve-o'clock news. The door was closed, and I opened it and entered, but two steps in I stopped. It was inhabited. Susan was in a chair, and standing facing her was a stranger, a man in a dark gray suit with a jaw that looked determined in profile. Evidently he had been too occupied to hear the door opening, for he didn't wheel to me until I had taken the two steps.

"Sorry," I said, "I'm just cruising," and was going, but Susan spoke.

"Don't go, Mr. Green. This is Jim Eber. Jim, this is Alan Green. You know he—I mentioned him."

My predecessor was still occupied, but not too much to lift a hand. I took it, and found that his muscles weren't interested. He spoke, not as if he wanted to. "I dropped in to see Mr. Jarrell, but he's away. Nothing important, just a little matter. How do you like the job?'

"I'd like it fine if it were all like the first two days. When Mr. Jarrell gets back, I don't know. I can try. Maybe you could give me some pointers."

"Pointers?"

You might have thought it was a word I had just made up. Obviously his mind wasn't on his vocabulary or on me; it was working on something, and not on getting his job back or I would have been a factor.

"Some other time," I said. "Sorry I interrupted."

"I was just going," he said, and, with his jaw set, marched past me and on out.

"Oh dear," Susan said.

I looked down at her. "I don't suppose there's anything I can help with?"

"No, thank you." She shook her head and her little oval face came up. Then she left the chair. "Do you mind? But of course you don't—only I don't want to be rude. I want to think something over."

I said something polite and she went. Eber had closed the door behind him and I opened it for her. She made for the rear and turned a corner, and in a moment I heard the elevator. With that settled, that she hadn't set out after Eber, I turned on the radio and got the tail end of the newscast.

That was the new acquaintance. The only other contribution that Wednesday made worth mentioning came six hours later, and though, as I said, it got me no farther along, it did add a new element to the situation. Before reporting it I should also mention my brief exchange with Wyman. I was in the lounge with a magazine when he appeared, stepped out to the terrace, came back in, and approached.

"You're not overworked, are you?" he asked.

There are several possible ways of asking that, running from the sneer to the brotherly smile. His was about in the middle. I might have replied, "Neither are you," but didn't. He was too skinny, and too handicapped by his tight little ears and thin straight nose, to make a good target, and besides, he thought he was trying. He had produced two shows on Broadway, and while one had folded after three days, the other had run nearly a month. Also his father had told me that in spite of the venomous influence of the snake he was still trying to teach him the technique of making money grow.

So I humored him. "No," I said.

The crease in his brow deepened. "You're not very talkative either."

"You're wrong there. When I get started I can talk your head off. For example. An hour ago I went into the studio to catch the newscast, and a man was there speaking with your wife, and she introduced me to him. It was Jim Eber. I'm wondering if he's trying to get his job back, and if so, whether he'll succeed. I left a good job to come here, and I don't want to find myself out on a limb. I don't want to ask your wife about it, and I'd appreciate it if you would ask her and let me know."

His lips had tightened, and he had become aware of it and had loosened them. "When was this? An hour ago?"

"Right. Just before noon."

"Were they talking about the—uh, about the job?"

"I don't know. I didn't know they were

there and I opened the door and went in. I thought he might have said something that would show if he's trying to get it back."

"Maybe he did."

"Will you ask her?"

"Yes. I'll ask her."

"I'll appreciate it a lot."

"I'll ask her." He turned, and turned back. "It's lunch time. You're joining us?"

I said I was.

There were only five of us at the table—Trella, Susan, Wyman, Roger, and Alan. Lois didn't show, and Nora lunched from a tray in the library. When, afterward, Roger invited me to his room, I thought the two hours before Jarrell arrived might as well be spent with him as with anyone. He won $2.43, and I deducted 92 cents and paid him $1.51. Wanting to save him the trouble of bringing up the Peach Fuzz project, I brought it up myself and told him the sixty bucks would be available that evening after dinner.

I was in the library with Nora when Jarrell returned, shortly after four o'clock. He breezed in, tossed his bag under a table, told Nora, "Get Clay," and went to his desk. Apparently I wasn't there. I sat and listened to his end of three phone conversa-

71

tions which I would have paid closer attention to if my name had been Alan Green. I did attend, with both ears, when I heard Nora, reporting on events during his absence, tell him that Jim Eber had called that morning.

His head jerked to her. "Called? Phoned?"

"No, he came. He got some papers he had left in his desk. He said that was what he came for. That was all. I looked at the papers; they were personal. Then he was with Susan in the studio; I don't know whether it was by appointment or not. Mr. Green was there with them when he left."

Evidently everybody knew everything around there. The fact that Eber had been there had been mentioned at the lunch table, but Nora hadn't been present. Of course any of the others might have told her, including Steck.

Jarrell snapped at me, "You were with them?"

I nodded. "Only briefly. I was going to turn on the radio for the news, and opened the door and went in. Your daughter-in-law introduced me to him and that was about all. He said he was just going and he went."

He opened his mouth and closed it again. Questions he might have asked Archie

Goodwin could not properly be asked Alan Green with the stenographer there. He turned to her. "What else did he want? Besides the papers."

"Nothing. That was all, except that he thought you would be here and wanted to see you. That's what he said."

He licked his lips, shot me a glance, and turned back to her. "All right, hand me the mail."

She got it from a drawer of her desk and took it to him. If you think it would have been natural for it to be on his desk waiting for him you're quite right, but in that case it would have been exposed to the view of the new secretary, and that wouldn't do. After sticking around a while longer I asked Jarrell if I was wanted, was told not until after dinner, and left them and went up to my room.

I can't tell you the exact minute that Jarrell came dashing in, yelling at me, but I can come close. It was a quarter to six when I decided to shower and shave before going down to the lounge for cocktails, and my par for that operation when I'm not pressed is half an hour, and I was pulling on my pants when the door flew open and he was there yapping. "Come on!" Seeing me, he was off down the hall, yapping again, "Come on!" It seemed that the occasion was informal enough not to demand socks and shoes, so I merely got my shirttail in, and fastened my belt and closed my zipper en route. I could hear him bounding down the stairs, and made for them and on down, and turned the corner just as he reached the library door. As I came up he tried the knob and then stood and stared at it.

"It's locked," he said.

"Why not?" I asked. "What's wrong?"

"Horland's phoned. He said the signal flashed and the screen showed the door opening and a blanket or rug coming in. He's sending a man. There's somebody in there. There must be."

"Then open the door."

"Horland's said to wait till his man got here."

"Nuts. I will." Then I realized I couldn't. My key, along with my other belongings, was up on the dresser. "Give me your key."

He got out his key fold and handed it to me, and I picked one and stuck it in the slot. "It's just possible," I said, "that we'll be rushed. Move over." He did so. I got behind the jamb, turned the key and the knob, pushed on the door with my bare

74

toes, and it swung open. Nothing happened. I said, "Stay here," and stepped inside. Nothing and no one. I went and took a look, behind desks, around corners of cabinets and shelves, in the closet, and in the bathroom. I was going to call him to come on in when the sound came of footsteps pounding down the corridor, and I reached the door in time to see the reinforcement arrive—a middle aged athlete in a gray uniform. He wasn't one that I knew. He was panting, and he had a gun in his hand.

"At ease," I commanded. "False alarm. Apparently. What's this about a blanket or a rug?"

"It's not a false alarm," Jarrell said. "I turned the switch on myself when I left, and the light didn't flash when you opened the door. Someone went in and turned the switch off. What was it you saw?"

Horland's didn't answer. He was looking at the floor at our feet. "By God, that's it," he said. He pointed. "That's it right there."

"What the hell are you talking about?" Jarrell blurted.

"That rug. That's what came in. The signal flashed and I looked at the screen, and in came that rug, hanging straight down, that was all I could see. Then it was gone, and in about two seconds the screen was dead. You get it? Someone came in holding that rug in front of him, and went and turned the switch off, and when he came out he put the rug back here where he got it. That's how I know he's not still in there; if he was, the rug wouldn't be here." He sounded as pleased as if he had just done a job of brain work that would be hard to match.

Thinking that a little pruning wouldn't hurt him, I asked, "How do you know it was this rug?"

"Why, the pattern. The squares, the lines crossing. I saw it."

"It might be one of a pair. He might be in there now, in the closet or the bathroom."

"Oh." He squared his shoulders. "Stand aside."

"Don't bother, I looked. He's gone. He didn't stay long." I turned to Jarrell. "You might try the switch. Go and turn it on and we'll enter."

He did so. After he was in I shut the door, and when he called to us I pushed it open, and the blaze of light came. I swung the door shut, and the light went, and we crossed to his desk.

"After you saw it on the screen, the rug coming in," I asked Horland's, "how long was it before you phoned?"

"Right away. No time at all. I didn't phone, the other man did, I told him to."

"How long did it take the call to get through?"

"It got through right away. I was putting on my cap and jacket and getting my gun, and I wasn't wasting any time, and he had Mr. Jarrell when I left."

"Then say thirty seconds. Make it a minute, not to skimp. Even two minutes. You answered the phone in your room, Mr. Jarrell?"

"Yes."

"How long were you on the phone?"

"Only long enough for him to tell me what had happened. Not more than a minute."

"And you came on the run immediately? Only stopping at my door on the way?"

"You're damn right I did."

"Then add another minute. That makes four minutes from the time the rug came in to the time we got here, and probably less, and he was gone. So he didn't have time for much more than turning off the switch."

"We ought to find out who it was," Horland's said. "While it's hot."

He certainly worked his brain, that bird. Obviously it had been a member of the household, and how and when to find out who it was was strictly a family affair. Jarrell didn't bother to tell him so. He merely gave him a chore, to unlock and open the door of a metal box that was set in the wall facing the entrance. Its door had a round hole for the lens to see through, and inside was the camera. Horland's took the camera out, extracted the film and put in a new one, returned the camera and locked the door and departed.

Jarrell regarded me. "You realize it could have been anybody. We may know more when we see the picture. But with that rug in front of her, she could have held it up high with her hands not showing, nothing at all showing, and you couldn't tell."

"Yes," I agreed, "she could. Anybody could. One pronoun is as good as another. As I said, she didn't have time for much more than turning off the switch, but you might look around. Is any little item missing?"

He moved his head from side to side, got up, went and tried the knobs of the safes, crossed to the battery of cabinets and pulled at the handles of the drawers in the two end tiers, which had locks on them, went and opened the top drawer of Nora Kent's desk and took a look, and then came back to his own desk and opened the top drawer of it. His face changed immediately. He pulled the drawer wide open, moved things around, and pushed it shut. He looked at me.

"Don't tell me," I said. "Let me guess."

He took a deep breath. "I keep a gun in there, a Bowdoin thirty-eight. It's gone. It was there this afternoon."

"Loaded?"

"Yes."

"Whoever got it knew you had it. He—I beg your pardon—she came straight to the desk, turned off the switch, grabbed the gun, and ran. That's all there was time for."

"Yes."

"Horland's was right about one thing. If you want to find out who it was, the sooner the better, while it's hot. The best way would be to get them all in here, now, and go to it."

"What good would that do?" His hands were fists. "I know who it was. So do you."

"I do not." I shook my head. "Look, Mr. Jarrell. Suspecting her of cheating your son and diddling you, without any evidence, that's your privilege. But saying that I know she came in here and took a loaded gun, when I don't, that is not your privilege. Of course you have a permit for it?"

"Certainly."

"The law says when a gun is stolen it must be reported. It's a misdemeanor not to. Do you want to report it?"

"Good God, no." The fists relaxed. "How about this? I'll get her in here, and Wyman too, and I'll keep them here while you go up and search their rooms. You know how to search a room."

One of two things, I thought. Either he is sure it was her, for some reason or no reason, or he took it himself and planted it in her room. "No good," I declared. "If she took it, the last place she would hide it would be in her room. I could find it, of course, in a couple of days, or much quicker if I got help in, but what if it turned up in one of the tubs on the terrace? You'd have the gun back, that's true, if that's what you want."

"You know damn well what I want."

"Yes, I ought to, but that's not the point now, or not the whole point. Anyone going to all that trouble and risk to get hold of a gun, he must—I beg your pardon—she must intend to use it for something. I doubt if it's to shoot a squirrel. It might even be to shoot you. I would resent that while I'm employed as your secretary. I advise you to get them in here and let me ask questions. Even better, take them all down to Mr. Wolfe and let him ask questions."

"No."

"You won't?"

"No."

"Then what?"

"I don't know. I'll see. I'll have to think." He looked at his wrist. "They're in the lounge." He stood up. "I'll see."

"Okay." I stood up. "I'd rather not appear barefooted. I'll go up and put on my shoes and socks."

As I said before, that added a new element to the situation.

―――――5――――――

WHEN Nero Wolfe came down from the plant rooms at six o'clock Thursday afternoon I was at my desk in the office, waiting for him. Growling a greeting, if you can call it that, as he crossed to his chair, he lowered his bulk and got it properly disposed, rested his elbows on the chair arms, and glared at me.

"Well?"

I had swiveled to him. "To begin with," I said, "as I told you on the phone, I'm not asking you to exert yourself if you'd rather not. I can hang on up there if it takes all summer, and with Orrie here you certainly don't need me. Only I didn't want you to have a client shot from under you with no warning from me. By the way, where is Orrie?"

"He stepped out. Who is going to shoot Mr. Jarrell?"

"I don't know. I don't even know he's going to be the target. Do you care to hear about it?"

"Go ahead."

I did so. Giving him only a sketchy outline of my encounters and experiences up to 6:15 p.m. Wednesday, when Jarrell had opened my door and yelled at me to come on, from there I made it more detailed. I reported verbatim my conversation with Jarrell after Horland's had gone.

Wolfe grunted. "The man's an ass. Every one of those people would profit by his death. They need a demonstration, or one of them does. He should have corralled them and called in the police to find the gun."

"Yeah. He's sure his daughter-in-law took it, or pretends he is. As I said on the phone Monday night, he may have an itch he can't reach and is not accountable. He could have pulled the rug act himself, answered the phone call from Horland's there in the library, raced upstairs to get me, and raced down again. He could have taken the gun earlier. I prefer it that way, since in that case there will probably be no bullets flying, but I admit it's not likely. He is not a nitwit."

"What has been done?"

"Nothing, actually. After dinner we played bridge, two tables—Trella, Lois, Nora, Jarrell, Wyman, Roger Foote, Corey Brigham, me. Incidentally, when I finally got down to the lounge before dinner Brigham was there with them, and I learned from Steck that he had come early, shortly after six o'clock, so I suppose it could have been him that got the gun, provided he had a key to the library. It was around midnight when we quit, and—"

"You didn't include the daughter-in-law."

"Haven't I mentioned that she doesn't play bridge? She doesn't. And we went to bed. Today I saw four of them at break-fast—Jarrell, Wyman, Lois and Nora—but not much of anybody since, except Susan and Trella at lunch. Jarrell mentioned at lunch that he would be out all afternoon, business appointments. At two-thirty, when I went around looking for company, they were all out. Of course Roger had gone to Jamaica, with the sixty bucks I gave him— by the way, I haven't entered that on the expense account. At three o'clock I went for a walk and phoned you, and when I got back there was still nobody at home except Nora, and she is no—oh, I forgot. The pictures."

"Pictures?"

"Sure, from the camera. A Horland's man brought them while I was out phoning you, and when I got back Nora had them. She wasn't sure whether she should let me look at them, but I was. That woman sure plays them close to her chin; I don't know now whether Jarrell had told her about the rug affair or not. If not, she must have won-dered what the pictures were all about. There were three of them; the camera takes one every two seconds until the door is shut. They all showed the rug broadside, coming straight in. He must have kicked the door shut. That rug is seven by three, so it could have been a tall man holding the top edge a little above the top of his head, or could have been a short woman holding it as high as she could reach. At the bottom the rug was just touching the floor. At the top its edge was turned back, hiding the hands. I was going to bring the pictures along to show you, but would have had to shoot Nora to get away with them. Jarrell wasn't back when I left at five-thirty."

I turned a hand over. "That's it. Any instructions?"

He made a face. "How the devil can I have instructions?"

"You might. For instance, instruct me to take Lois out tonight. Or take Trella to lunch tomorrow. Or stick around until Sunday and take Susan to church."

"Phui. Give me a plain answer for once. How likely is it that you'll accomplish anything up there?"

"One in a million, if you mean fairly soon. Give me until Thanksgiving and I might show you something. However, there's one little teaser. Its name is Eber, James L. Eber. He was upset about something when I found him in the studio with Susan, and so was she. Wyman was upset

85

when I told him Eber had been there. When it was mentioned at the lunch table Roger was upset, and maybe one or two of the others. Jarrell was upset when Nora told him about it. And it was only an hour or so later that the gun was taken. There might be something to be pried out of Eber. I've been prying for three days without breaking off a splinter, and as a last resort he might have one loose. He just might have something interesting to say to the guy who took his job."

He grunted. "I doubt if any of those people has anything interesting to say to anyone."

I said I did too but that Eber should have a chance and I would go and give him one after dinner.

Orrie Cather dined with us. I went upstairs two flights to tell my room hello, and when I went back down Orrie was there, and we had time to exchange some friendly insults before Fritz announced dinner. The main dish was shad roe with créole sauce. Shad roe is all right, and Fritz's créole sauce is one of the best, but the point is that with that item Fritz always serves bread triangles fried in anchovy butter; and since he had known four hours ago that I would be there, and he was aware of my attitude toward bread triangles fried in anchovy butter, he had proceeded beyond the call of duty. Again I passed up a salad, but only because there wasn't room for it.

Back in the office, with coffee, Orrie, who had been told that I was going on an errand, asked if I needed any help, and I said I hoped not. When he saw me getting a ring of keys from a drawer he said I might need a lookout, and I repeated that I hoped not. When he saw me getting a shoulder holster and a gun from another drawer he said I might need a loader, and I told him he ought to know better, that if six wasn't enough what I would need would be a meat basket to bring me home in.

I had no reason to think there would be any occasion for the gun, but ever since Jarrell had opened the drawer and found his gone I had felt unfurnished. A man who—I beg your pardon—a woman who steals a loaded gun deserves to be treated with respect. As for the keys, they were routine equipment when calling on a stranger who might have useful information and who might or might not be home. There would probably be no occasion for them either, but I dislike waiting in dark halls with nothing to sit on.

The address, which I got from my notebook, on 49th Street between Second and Third Avenues, was above the door of an old five-story building that was long past its glory if it had ever had any. In the vestibule, I found EBER in the middle of the row of names, and pushed the button. No click. I pushed it five times, with waits in between, before giving up. I certainly wasn't going to do my waiting there, if any, and the old Manson lock was no problem, so I got out the keys, selected one, and in less than a minute was inside. If the position of his name in the row was correct he was two flights up, and he was—or his name was, on the jamb of a door in the rear, with a button beside it. When I pushed the button I could hear the ring inside.

I was in the dark hall with nothing to sit on that I don't like to wait in. Since there might be some information inside, in some form or other, that I could get more easily with him not there, I was sorry I hadn't brought Orrie along, because with a lookout there would have been nothing to it, but in three minutes I was glad I hadn't. That was how long it took me to decide to go on in, to get the lock worked, to enter, to see him sprawled on the floor, and to check that he was dead. Then I was glad Orrie hadn't come.

He was backside up, so I didn't have to disturb him in order to see the hole in the back of his head, a little below the center. When I spread the hair it looked about the right size for a .38, but I wasn't under oath. Standing up, I looked around, all the way around. There was no gun in sight, and it couldn't very well be under him. I didn't have to sniff to get the smell of powder, but there were no open windows, so it would take it a while to go.

I stood and considered. Had I been seen by anybody who might identify me later? Possibly, but I doubted it. Certainly by no one inside, or even in the vestibule. Was it worth the risk to give the dump a good going over to see what I could find? Maybe; but I had no gloves, and everything there would be tried for prints; and it would be embarrassing if someone came before I left. Had I touched anything besides his hair? You can touch something without knowing it—the top of a table, for instance, as you cross a room. I decided I hadn't.

It was a pity that I had to wipe the door

knob and the surface around the keyhole outside, since there might be prints there that Homicide could use, but there was no help for it. I did it thoroughly but quickly. I hadn't liked the idea of hanging around the hall before, and I liked it much less now. At the top of the stairs I listened three seconds, and, descending, did the same on the next landing. My luck held, and I was down, out to the sidewalk, and on my way without anyone to notice me. I was thinking that items of routine that become automatic through habit, though they are usually wasted, can be very useful—for instance, my having the taxi drop me at 49th Street and Third Avenue instead of taking me to the address. Now, not caring to have anything at all to do with a taxi on the East Side, I walked crosstown all the way to Ninth Avenue before flagging one. I needed a little walk anyway, to jolt my brain back into place. It had been 8:57 when I had stood up after looking at the hole in Jim Eber's head. It was 9:28 when the taxi pulled up at the curb in front of the old brownstone on West 35th Street.

When I entered the office Orrie was in one of the yellow chairs over by the big globe, with a magazine. I noted that with approval, since it showed that he fully appreciated the fact that my desk was mine. At sight of me Wolfe, behind his desk with a book, dropped his eyes back to the page. I hadn't been gone long enough to get much of a splinter.

I tossed my hat on my desk and sat. "I have a comment to make about the weather," I said, "privately. Orrie hates to hear the weather mentioned. Don't you, Orrie?"

"I sure do." He got up, closing the magazine. "I can't stand it. If you touch on anything you think I'd be interested in, whistle." He went, closing the door behind him.

Wolfe was scowling at me. "What is it now?"

"A vital statistic. Ringing James L. Eber's bell several times and getting no reaction, and finding the door was locked, I used a key and entered. He was on the floor face down in the middle of the room, with a bullet hole in the back of his head which could have been made by a thirty-eight. He was cooling off, but not cold. I would say, not for quotation, that he had been dead from three to seven hours. As you know, that depends. I did no investigating because

I didn't care to stay. I don't think I was seen entering or leaving."

Wolfe's lips had tightened until he practically didn't have any. "Preposterous," he said distinctly.

"What is?" I demanded. "It's not preposterous that he's dead, with that hole in his skull."

"This whole affair. You shouldn't have gone there in the first place."

"Maybe not. You suggested it."

"I did not suggest it. I raised difficulties."

I crossed my legs. "If you want to try to settle that now," I said, "okay, but you know how things like that drag on, and I need instructions. I should have called headquarters and told them where to find something interesting but didn't, because I thought you might possibly have a notion."

"I have no notion and don't intend to have one," Wolfe said.

"Then I'll call. From a booth. They say they can't trace a local dial call, but there might be a miracle. Next, do I get back up there quick, I mean to Jarrell's, and if so what's my line?"

"I said I have no notion. Why should you go back there at all?"

I uncrossed my legs. "Look," I said, "you might as well come on down. I could go back just to return his ten grand and tell him we're bowing out, if that's what you want, but it's not quite so simple and you know it. When the cops learn that Eber was Jarrell's secretary and got fired, they'll be there asking questions. If they learn that Jarrell hired you and you sent me to take his place—don't growl at me, they'll think you sent me no matter what you think—you know what will happen, they'll be on our necks. Even if they don't learn that, we have a problem. We know that a thirty-eight revolver was taken from Jarrell's desk yesterday afternoon, and we know that Eber was there yesterday morning and it made a stir, and if and when we also know that the bullet that killed him came from a thirty-eight, what do we do, file it and forget it?"

He grunted. "There is no obligation to report what may be merely a coincidence. If Mr. Jarrell's gun is found and it is established that Eber was killed by a bullet from it, that will be different."

"Meanwhile we ignore the coincidence?"

"We don't proclaim it."

"Then I assume we keep the ten grand and Jarrell is still your client. If he turns out to be a murderer, what the hell, many law-yers' clients are murderers. And I'm back where I started, I need instructions. I'll have to go—"

The phone rang. I swiveled and got it, and I noticed that Wolfe reached for his too, which he rarely does unless I give him a sign.

"Nero Wolfe's residence, Archie Goodwin speaking."

"Where the hell are you? This is Jarrell."

"You know what number you dialed, Mr. Jarrell. I'm with Mr. Wolfe, reporting and getting instructions about your job."

"I've got instructions for you myself. Nora says you left at five-thirty. You've been gone over four hours. How soon can you be here?"

"Oh, say in an hour."

"I'll be in the library."

He hung up. I cradled it and turned.

"He reminds me of you a little," I said—just an interesting fact, nothing personal. "I was about to say, I'll have to go back up there and I need to know what for. Just hang around or try to start something? For instance, it would be a cinch to put the bee on Jarrell. You couldn't ask for a better setup for blackmail. I tell him that if he

94

makes a sizeable contribution in cash, say half a million, we'll regard the stolen gun as a coincidence and forget it. If he doesn't, we'll feel that we must report it. Of course I'll have to wait until the news is out about Eber, but if—"

"Shut up."

"Yes, sir."

He eyed me. "You understand the situation. You have expounded it."

"Yes, sir."

"This may or may not affect the job you undertook for Mr. Jarrell—don't interrupt me—very well, that *we* undertook. Murder sometimes creates only ripples, but more frequently high seas. Assuredly you are not going back there to take women to lunch at Rusterman's or to taverns to dance. I offer no complaint for what has been done; I will concede that we blundered into this mess by a collaboration in mulishness; but if it was Mr. Jarrell's gun that was used to kill Eber, and it isn't too fanciful to suppose that it was, we are in it willy-nilly, and we should emerge, if not with profit, at least without discomfiture. That is our joint concern. You ask if you should start something up there. I doubt if you'll need to; something has already started. It is most likely that the murder had no connection with that hive of predators and parasites. I can't tell you how to proceed because you'll have to wait on events. You will be guided by your intelligence and experience, and report to me as the occasion dictates. Mr. Jarrell said he has instructions for you. Have you any notion what they'll be?"

"Not a glimmer."

"Then we can't anticipate them. You will call police headquarters?"

"Yes, on my way."

"That will expedite matters. Otherwise there's no telling when the body would be found."

I was on my feet. "If you phone me there," I told him, "keep it decent. He has four phones on his desk, and I suspect two of them."

"I won't phone you. You'll phone me."

"Okay," I said, and went.

6

PASSING the gauntlet of the steely eyes of the lobby sentinel, mounting in the private elevator, and using my key in the tenth-floor vestibule, I found that the electronic security apparatus hadn't been switched on yet. Steck appeared, of course, and said Mr. Jarrell would like to see me in the library. The eye I gave him was a different eye from what it had been. It could even have been Steck who had worked the rug trick to get hold of a gun. He had his duties, but he might have managed to squeeze it in.

Hearing voices in the lounge, I crossed the reception hall to glance in, and saw Trella, Nora and Roger Foote at a card table.

Roger looked up and called to me. "Pinochle! Come and take a hand!"

"Sorry, I can't. Mr. Jarrell wants me."

"Come when you're through! Peach Fuzz ran a beautiful race! Beautiful! Five lengths back at the turn and only a head behind at the finish! Beautiful!"

A really fine loser, I was thinking as I headed for the corridor. You don't often meet that kind of sporting spirit. Beautiful!

The door of the library was standing open. Entering, I closed it. Jarrell, over by the files with one of the drawers open, barked at me, "Be with you in a minute," and I went to the chair at an end of his desk. A Portanaga with an inch of ash intact was there on a tray, and the smell told me it was still alive, so it couldn't have been more than ninety seconds since he left his desk to go to the files. That's the advantage of being a detective with a trained mind; you collect all kinds of useless facts without even trying.

He came and sat, picked up the cigar and tapped the ash off, and took a couple of puffs. He spoke. "Why did you go to see Wolfe?"

"He pays my salary. He likes to know what he's getting for it. Also I told him on the phone about your gun disappearing, and he wanted to ask me about it."

"Did you have to tell him about that?"

"I thought I'd better. You're his client, and he doesn't like to have his clients shot, and if somebody used the gun to kill you with and I hadn't told him about it he would have been annoyed. Besides, I thought he might want to make a suggestion."

"Did he make one?"

"Not a suggestion exactly. He made a comment. He said you're an ass. He said you should have corralled everybody and got the cops in to find the gun."

"Did you tell him I'm convinced that my daughter-in-law took it?"

"Sure. But even if she did, and if she

intends to use it on you, that would still be the best way to handle it. It would get the gun back, and it would notify her that you haven't got a hole in your head and don't intend to have one."

He showed no reaction to my mentioning a hole in the head. "It was you who said we'd probably find it in a tub on the terrace."

"I didn't say probably, but what if I did? We'd have the gun. You said on the phone you've got instructions for me. About looking for it?"

"No, not that." He took a pull on the cigar, removed it, and let the smoke float out. "I don't remember just how much I've told you about Corey Brigham."

"Not much. No details. That he's an old friend of yours—no, you didn't use the word friend—that he got in ahead of you on a deal, and that you think your daughter-in-law was responsible. I've been a little surprised to see him around."

"I want him around. I want him to think I've accepted his explanation and I don't suspect anything. The deal was about a shipping company. I found out about a claim that could be made against it, and I was all set to buy the claim and then put the screws on, and when I was ready to close in I found that Brigham was there ahead of me. He said he got next to it through somebody else, that he didn't know I was after it, but he's a damn liar. There wasn't anybody else. The only source was mine, and I had it clamped tight. He got it through information that was in this room, and he got it from my daughter-in-law."

"That raises questions," I told him. "I don't have to ask why Susan gave it to him because I already know your answer to that. She gives things to men, including her—uh, favors, because that's what she's like. But how did she get it?"

"She got my gun yesterday, didn't she?"

"I don't know and neither do you. Anyhow, how many times has that rug walked in here?"

"Not any. That was a new one. But she knows how to find a way to get anything she wants. She could have got it from Jim Eber. Or from my son. Or she could have been in here with my son when Nora and I weren't here, and sent him out for something, and got it herself. God only knows what else she got. Most of my operations are based on some kind of inside information, and a lot of it is on paper, it has to be, and I'm afraid to leave anything important in here any more. Goddamn it, she has to go!"

He pulled at the cigar, found it was out, and dropped it in the tray. "There's another aspect. I stood to clear a million on that deal, probably more. So Brigham did instead of me, and she got her share of it. She gives things to men, including her favors if you want to call it that, but all the time her main object is herself. She got her share. That's what I've got instructions about. See if you can find it. She's got it salted away somewhere and maybe you can find it. Maybe you can get a lead to it through Brigham. Get next to him. He's a goddamn snob, but he won't be snooty to my secretary if you handle him right. Another possibility is Jim Eber. Get next to him too. You met him yesterday. I don't know just what your approach will be, but you should be able to work that out yourself. And don't forget our deal—yours and mine. Ten thousand the day she's out of here, with my son staying, and fifty thousand when the divorce papers are signed."

I had been wondering if he had forgotten about that. I was also wondering if he figured that later, remembering that he had told me Thursday night to get next to Jim Eber, I would regard that as evidence that he hadn't been aware that Eber was no longer approachable.

I reminded him that it takes two to make a deal and that I hadn't accepted his offer, but he waved that away as not worth discussing. His suggestion that I cultivate Eber made it relevant for me to ask questions about him, and I did so, but while some of the answers I got might have been helpful for getting to know him better, none of them shed any light on the most important fact about him, that he was dead. He had been with Jarrell five years, unmarried, was a Presbyterian but didn't work at it, played golf on Sunday, was fair to good at bridge, and so on. I also collected some data on Corey Brigham.

When Jarrell finished with me and I went, leaving him at his desk, I stood outside for a moment, on the rug that walked like a man, or a woman, debating whether to go and join the pinochle players, to observe them from the new angle I now had on the whole bunch, or to go for a walk and call Wolfe to tell him what Jarrell's instructions had been. It was a draw, so I decided to do neither and went upstairs to bed.

I slept all right, I always sleep, but woke up at seven o'clock. I turned over and shut my eyes again, but nothing doing. I was awake. It was a damn nuisance. I would have liked to get up and dress and go down to the studio and hear the eight o'clock news. It had been exactly ten-thirty when I had phoned headquarters to tell them, in falsetto, that they had better take a look at a certain apartment at a certain number on 49th Street, and by now the news would be out and I wanted to hear it. But on Tuesday I had appeared for breakfast at 9:25, on Wednesday at 10:15, and on Thursday at 9:20, and if I shattered precedent by show-ing before eight, making for the radio, and announcing what I had heard to anyone available—and it would be remarkable not to announce it—someone might have won-dered how come. So when my eyes wouldn't stay closed no matter which side I tried, I lay on my back and let them stay open, hoping they liked the ceiling. They didn't. They kept turning—up, down, right, left. I got the impression that they were trying to turn clear over to see inside. When I found myself wondering what would happen if they actually made it I decided that had gone far enough, kicked the sheet off, and got up.

I took my time in the shower, and shaving, and putting cuff links in a clean shirt, and other details; and history repeated itself. I was pulling on my pants, getting the second leg through, when there was a knock at the door, and nothing timid about it. I called out, "Who is it?", and for reply the door opened, and Jarrell walked in.

I spoke. "Good morning. Come some time when I've got my shoes on."

He had closed the door. "This can't wait. Jim Eber is dead. They found his body in his apartment. Murdered. Shot."

I stared, not overdoing it. "For God's sake. When?"

"I got it on the radio—the eight o'clock news. They found him last night. He was shot in the head, in the back. That's all it said. It didn't mention that he worked for me." He went to a chair, the big one by the window, and sat. "I want to discuss it with you."

I had put my shoes and clean socks by that chair, intending to sit there to put them on. Going to get them, taking another chair, pulling my pants leg up, and starting a sock on, I said, "If they don't already know he worked for you they soon will, you realize that."

"Certainly I realize it. They may phone, or come, any minute. That's what I want to discuss."

I picked up the other sock. "All right, discuss. Shoot."

"You know what a murder investigation is like, Goodwin. You know that better than I do."

"Yeah. It's no fun."

"It certainly isn't. Of course they may already have a line on somebody, they may even have the man that did it, there was nothing on the radio about that. But if they haven't, and if they don't get him soon, you know what it will be like. They'll dig everywhere as deep as they can. He was with me five years, and he lived here. They'll want to know everything about him, and it's mostly here they'll expect to get it."

I was tying a shoelace. "Yeah, they have no respect for privacy, when it's murder."

He nodded. "I know they haven't. And I know the best way to handle it is to tell them anything they want to know, within reason. If they think I'm holding out that will only make it worse, I appreciate that. One thing I want to discuss with you, they'll ask why I fired Eber, and what do I say?"

I had my shoes on now and was on equal

terms. Conferring in bare feet with a man who is properly shod may not put you at a disadvantage, but it seems to. It may be because he could step on your toes. With mine now protected, I said, "Just tell them why you fired him. That you suspected him of leaking business secrets."

He shook his head. "If I do that they'll want details—what secrets he leaked and who to, all that. That would take them onto ground where I don't want them. I would rather tell them that Eber was getting careless, he seemed to be losing interest, and I decided to let him go. No matter what else they ask, nobody could contradict that, not even Nora, except one person. You. If they ask you, you can simply say that you don't know much about it, that you understand that I was dissatisfied with Eber but you don't know why. Can't you?"

I was frowning at him. "This must have given you quite a jolt, Mr. Jarrell. You'd better snap out of it. Two of Mr. Wolfe's oldest and dearest enemies, and mine, are Inspector Cramer and Sergeant Stebbins of Homicide. The minute they catch sight of me and learn that I'm here under another name in Eber's job, the sparks will start flying. No matter what reason you give them for firing him they won't believe you. They won't believe me. They won't believe anybody. The theory they'll like best will be that you decided that Eber had to be shot and got me in as a technical consultant. That may be stretching it a little, but it gives you an idea."

"Good God." He was stunned. "Of course."

"So I can't simply say I don't know much about it."

"Good God no. My mind wasn't working." He leaned forward at me. "Look, Goodwin. The other thing I was going to ask, I was going to ask you to say nothing about what happened Wednesday—about my gun being taken. I'm not afraid that gun was used to shoot Eber, that's not it, it may not have been that caliber, but when they come here on a murder investigation you know how it will be if they find out that my gun was stolen just the day before. And if it was that caliber it will be a hundred times worse. So I was going to ask you not to mention it. Nobody else knows about it. Horland's man doesn't. He left before I found it was gone."

"I told you I told Mr. Wolfe."

"They don't have to get to Wolfe."

"Maybe they don't have to but they will, as soon as they see me. I'll tell you, Mr. Jarrell, it seems to me you're still jolted. You're not thinking straight. The way you feel about your daughter-in-law, this may be right in your lap. You want to sink her so bad you can taste it. You hired Mr. Wolfe and gave him ten thousand dollars for a retainer, and then offered me another sixty thousand. If you tell Inspector Cramer all about it—only Cramer, not Stebbins or Rowcliff or any of his gang, and not some squirt of an assistant district attorney—and tell him about the gun, and he starts digging at it and comes up with proof that Susan shot Eber, what better could you ask? You said you knew Susan took the gun, and if so she wanted to use it on someone, and why not Eber? And if you're afraid Cramer might botch it, keep Mr. Wolfe on the job. He loves to see to it that Cramer doesn't botch something."

"No," he said positively.

"Why not? You'll soon know if Eber was shot with a thirty-eight. I can find out about that for you within an hour, as soon as I get some breakfast. Why not?"

"I won't have them—I won't do it. No. You know damn well I won't. I won't tell the police about my personal affairs and have them spread all over. I don't want you or Wolfe telling them, either. I see now that my idea wouldn't work, that if they find out you're here in Eber's place there'll be hell to pay. So they won't find out. You won't be here, and you'd better leave right now because they might come any minute. If they want to know where my new secretary is I'll take care of that. He has only been here four days and knew nothing about Eber. You'd better leave now."

"And go where?"

"Where you belong, damn it!" He gestured, a hand out. "You'll have to make allowances for me, Goodwin. I've had a jolt, certainly I have. If you're not here and if I account for the absence of my new secretary, they'll never get to you or Wolfe either. Tell Wolfe I'm still his client and I'll get in touch with him. He said he was discreet. Tell him there's no limit to what his discretion may be worth to me."

He left the chair. "As for you, no limit with you too. I'm a tough operator, but I pay for what I get. Go on, get your necktie on. Leave your stuff here, that won't matter, you can get it later. We understand each other, don't we?"

"If we don't we will."

"I like you, Goodwin. Get going."

I moved. He stood and watched me while I got my tie and jacket on, gathered a few items and put them in the small bag, and closed the bag. When I glanced back as I turned the corner at the end of the hall, he was standing in front of the door of my room. I was disappointed not to see Steck in the corridor or reception hall; he must have had morning duties somewhere. Outside, I crossed the avenue, flagged a taxi headed downtown, and at a quarter past nine was mounting the stoop of the old brownstone. Wolfe would be up in the plant rooms for his morning session, from nine to eleven, with the orchids.

The chain bolt was on, so I had to ring, and it was Orrie Cather who opened up. He extended a hand. "Take your bag, sir?"

I let him take it, strode down the hall to the kitchen, and pushed the door.

Fritz, at the sink, turned. "Archie! A pleasure! You're back?"

"I'm back for breakfast, anyhow. My God, I'm empty! No orange juice even. One dozen pancakes, please."

I did eat seven.

I was in the office, refreshed and refueled, in time to get the ten o'clock news. It didn't add much to what Jarrell had heard two hours earlier, and nothing that I didn't already know.

Orrie, at ease on the couch, inquired, "Did it help any? I'm ignorant, so I have to ask. What's hot, the budget?"

"Yeah, I'm underwriting it. I'm also writing a book on criminology and researching it. Excuse me, I'm busy."

I dialed a number I didn't have to look up, the *Gazette,* asked for Lon Cohen's extension, and in a minute had him.

"Lon? Archie. I'm col—"

"I'm busy."

"So am I. I'm collecting data for a book. What did you shoot James L. Eber with, an arquebus?"

"No, my arquebus is in hock. I used a flintlock. What is it to you?"

"I'm just curious. If you'll satisfy my curiosity I'll satisfy yours some day. Have they found the bullet?"

Lon is a fine guy and a good poker player, but he has the occupational disease of all journalists: before he'll answer a question he has to ask one. So he did. "Has Wolfe got a thumb in it already?"

"Not a thumb, a foot. No, he hasn't, not for the record. If and when, you first as usual. Have they found the bullet?"

"Yes. It just came in. A thirty-eight, that's all so far. Who is Wolfe's client?"

"J. Edgar Hoover. Have they arrested anybody?"

"No. My God, give 'em time to sweep up and sit down and think. It was only twelve hours ago. I've been thinking ever since I heard your voice just now. What I think, I think it was you who called headquarters last night and told them to go and look, and I'm sore. You should have called me first."

"I should, at that. Next time. Have they or you or anyone got any kind of a lead?"

"To the murderer, no. So far the most interesting item is that up to a couple of weeks ago he was working for a guy named Otis Jarrell, you know who he is—*by God!* It was him you phoned me the other day to get dope on!"

"Sure it was. That's one reason—"

"Is Jarrell Wolfe's client?"

"For the present, as far as I'm concerned, Wolfe has no client. I was saying, that's one reason I'm calling now. I thought you might remember I had asked about him, and I wanted to tell you not to trust your memory until further notice. Just go ahead and gather the news and serve the public. You may possibly hear from me some day."

"Come on up here. I'll buy you a lunch."

"I can't make it, Lon. Sorry. Don't use any wooden bullets."

As I pushed the phone back Orrie asked, "What's an arquebus?"

"Figure it out yourself. A combination of an ark and a bus. Amphibian."

"Then don't." He sat up. "If I'm not supposed to be in on whatever you think you're doing, okay, but I have a right to know what an arquebus is. Do you want me out of here?"

I told him no, I could think better with him there for contrast.

But he got bounced when Wolfe came down at eleven o'clock. From the kitchen I had buzzed the plant rooms on the house phone to tell him I was there, so he wasn't surprised to see me. He went to his desk, glanced at the morning mail, which was skimpy, straightened his desk blotter, and focused on me. "Well?"

"In my opinion," I said, "the time has come for a complete report."

His eyes went over my shoulder to the couch. "If we need you on this, Orrie, you will get all the required information. That can wait."

"Yes, sir." Orrie got up and went.

When the door had closed behind him I spoke. "I called Lon Cohen. The bullet that killed Eber is a thirty-eight. Jarrell didn't know that when he entered my room this morning, knocking but not waiting for an invitation. He only knew what he had heard on the radio at eight o'clock, and I suppose you heard it too. Even so, he badly needed a tranquilizer. When I report in full you'll know what he said. It ended with his telling me to beat it quick before the cops arrived. He said to tell you he's still your client and he'll get in touch with you, and there's no limit to what your discretion may be worth to him. Me too. My discretion is as good as yours. Now that I know it was a thirty-eight, I have only two alternatives. Either I go down to Homicide and open the bag, or I give you the whole works from the beginning, words and music, and you listen, and then put your mind on it. If I get tossed in the coop for withholding evidence you can't operate anyhow, with me not here to supervise, so you might as well be with me."

"Pfui. As I said last night, there is no obligation to report what may be merely a coincidence." He sighed. "However, I concede that I'll have to listen. As for putting my mind on it, we'll see. Go ahead."

It took me two hours. I will not say that I gave him every word that had been pronounced in my hearing since Monday afternoon, four days back, but I came close to it. I left out some of Tuesday evening at Colonna's with Lois; things that are said between dances, when the band is good and your partner is better than good, are apt to be irrelevant and off key in a working detective's report. Aside from that I didn't miss much, and nothing of any importance, and neither did he. If he listens at all, he listens. The only interruptions were the two bottles of beer he rang for, brought by Fritz—both, of course, for Wolfe. The last half hour he was leaning back in his chair with his eyes closed, but that didn't mean he wasn't getting it.

I stood up and stretched and sat down

again. "So what it amounts to is that we are to sit it out, nothing to do but eat and sleep, and name our figure."

"Not an intolerable lot, Archie. The figure you suggested last evening was half a million."

"Yes, sir. I've decided that Billy Graham wouldn't approve. Say that the chance is one in ten that one of them killed Eber. I think it's at least fifty-fifty, but even if it's only one in ten I pass. So do you. You have to. You know darned well it's one of two things. One is to call it off with Jarrell, back clear out, and hand it over to Cramer. He would appreciate it."

He made a face. His eyes opened. "What's the other?"

"You go to work."

"At what? Investigating the murder of Mr. Eber? No one has hired me to."

I grinned at him. "No good. You call it quibbling, I call it dodging. The murder is in only because one of them might have done it, with Jarrell's gun. The question is, do we tell Cramer about the gun. We would rather not. The client would rather not. The only way out, if we're not going to tell Cramer, is to find out if one of them killed Eber—not to satisfy a judge and jury, just

116

to satisfy us. If they didn't, to hell with Cramer. If they did, we go on from there. The only way to find out is for you to go to work, and the only way for you to get to work is for me to phone Jarrell and tell him to have them here, all of them, at six o'clock today. What's wrong with that?"

"You would," he growled.

"Yes, sir. Of course there's a complication: me. To them I'm Alan Green, so I can't be here as Archie Goodwin, but that's easy. Orrie can be Archie Goodwin, at my desk, and I'll be Alan Green. Since I was in on the discovery that the gun was gone, I should be present." I looked up at the wall clock. "Lunch in eight minutes. I should phone Jarrell right now."

I made it slow motion, taking ten seconds to swivel, pull the phone over, lift the receiver, and start dialing, to give him plenty of time to stop me. He didn't. How could he, after my invincible logic? Nor did he move to take his phone.

Then a voice was in my ear. "Mr. Otis Jarrell's office."

It wasn't Nora, but a male, and I thought I knew what male. I said I was Alan Green and wanted to speak to Mr. Jarrell, and in a moment had him.

"Yes, Green?"

I kept my voice down. "Is anyone else on?"

"No."

"You're sure?"

"Yes."

"Was that Wyman answering?"

"Yes."

"He's there in the office with you?"

"Yes."

"Then you'd better let me do the talking and stick to yes and no. I'm here with Mr. Wolfe. Do you know that the bullet that killed Eber is a thirty-eight?"

"No."

"Well, it is. Have you had any callers?"

"Yes."

"Anything drastic?"

"No."

"Ring me later and tell me about it if you want to. I'm calling for Mr. Wolfe. Now that we know it was a thirty-eight, he thinks I should tell the police about your gun. It could be a question of withholding evidence. He feels strongly about it, but he is willing to postpone it, on one condition. The condition is that you have everybody in this office at six o'clock today so he can question them. By everybody he means you, your wife,

Wyman, Susan, Lois, Nora Kent, Roger Foote, and Corey Brigham. I'll be here as Alan Green, your secretary. Another man will be at my desk as Archie Goodwin."

"I don't see how—"

"Hold it. I know you're biting nails, but hold it. You can tell them that Mr. Wolfe will explain why this conference is necessary, and he will. Have you told any of them about your gun being taken?"

"No."

"Don't. He will. He'll explain that when you learned that Eber had been shot with a thirty-eight—that should be on the air by now, and it will be in the early afternoon papers—you were concerned, naturally, and you hired him to investigate, and he insisted on seeing all of you. I know you've got objections. You'll have to swallow them, but if you want help on it get rid of Wyman and Nora and call me back. If you don't call me back we'll be expecting you, all of you, here at six o'clock."

"No. I'll call back."

"Sure, glad to have you."

I hung up, turned, and told Wolfe, "You heard all of it except his noes and yeses. Satisfactory?"

"No," he said, but that was just reflex.

119

I'll say one thing for Wolfe, he hates to have anyone else's meals interrupted almost as much as his own. One of the standing rules in that house is that when we are at table, and nothing really hot is on, Fritz answers the phone in the kitchen, and if it seems urgent I go and get it. There may be something or somebody Wolfe would leave the table for, but I don't know what or who.

That day Fritz was passing a platter of what Wolfe calls hedgehog omelet, which tastes a lot better than it sounds, when the phone rang, and I told Fritz not to bother and went to the office. It was Jarrell calling back, and he had a lot of words besides yes and no. I permitted him to let off steam until it occurred to me that the omelet would be either cold or shriveled, and then told him firmly that it was either bring them or else. Back at the table I found that the omelet had no chance to either cool or shrivel, not with Orrie there to help Wolfe with it. I did get a bite.

We had just started on the avocado, whipped with sugar and lime juice and green chartreuse, when the doorbell rang. During meals Fritz was supposed to get that too, but I thought Jarrell might have rushed down to use more words face to face, so I got up and went to the hall for a look through the one-way glass panel in the front door. Having looked, I returned to the dining room and told Wolfe, "One's here already. The stenographer, Nora Kent."

He swallowed avocado. "Nonsense. You said six o'clock."

"Yes, sir. She must be on her own." The bell rang again. "And she wants in." I aimed a thumb at Orrie. "Archie Goodwin here can take her to the office and shut the door."

"Confound it." He was going to have to work sooner than expected. To Orrie: "You are Archie Goodwin."

"Yes, sir," Orrie said. "It's a comedown, but I'll try. Do I know her?"

"No. You have never seen or heard of her." The bell rang again. "Take her to the office and come and finish your lunch."

He went. He closed the door, but the office was just across the hall, and it might startle her if she heard Alan Green's voice as she went by, so I used my mouth for an avocado depot only. Sounds came faintly, since the walls and doors on that floor are all soundproofed.

When Orrie entered he shut the door, returned to his place, picked up his spoon, and spoke. "You didn't say to rub it in that

I'm Archie Goodwin, and she didn't ask, so I didn't mention it. She said her name was Nora Kent, and she wants to see Mr. Wolfe. How long am I going to be Archie Goodwin?"

I put in. "Mr. Wolfe never talks business at the table, you know that, Orrie. You haven't been told yet, but you were going to be me at a party later on, and now you can practice. Just sit at my desk and look astute. I'll have my eye on you. I'll be at the hole—unless Mr. Wolfe has other plans."

"No," Wolfe muttered. "I have no plans."

The hole, ten inches square, was at eye level in the wall twelve feet to the right of Wolfe's desk. On the office side it was covered by what appeared to be just a pretty picture of a waterfall. On the other side, in a wing of the hall across from the kitchen, it was covered by nothing, and you could not only see through but also hear through. My longest stretch there was one night when we had four people in the front room waiting for Wolfe to show up (he was in the kitchen chinning with Fritz), and we were expecting and hoping that one of them would sneak into the office to get something from a drawer of Wolfe's desk, and we wanted to know which one. That time I stood there at that hole more than three hours, and the door from the front room never opened.

This time it was much less than three hours. Orrie waited to open the door to the office until I was around the corner to the wing, so I saw his performance when they went in. As Goodwin he was barely adequate introducing Wolfe to her, hamming it, I thought; and crossing to my desk and sitting, he was entirely out of character, no grace or flair at all. I would have to rehearse him before six o'clock came. I had a good view of him and Nora, but could get Wolfe, in profile, only by sticking my nose into the hole and pressing my forehead against the upper edge.

WOLFE: I'm sorry you had to wait, Miss Kent. It is *Miss* Kent?

NORA: Yes. I am employed by Mr. Otis Jarrell. His stenographer. I believe you know him.

WOLFE: There is no taboo on beliefs, or shouldn't be. The right to believe will be the last to go. Proceed.

NORA: You do know Mr. Jarrell?

WOLFE: My dear madam. I have rights too—for instance, the right to decline inquisition by a stranger. You are not here by appointment.

(That was meant to cut. If it did, no blood showed.)

NORA: There wasn't time to make one. I had to see you at once. I had to ask you why you sent your confidential assistant, Archie Goodwin, to take a job with Mr. Jarrell as his secretary.

WOLFE: I wasn't aware that I had done so. Archie, did I send you to take a job as Mr. Jarrell's secretary?

ORRIE: No, sir, not that I remember.

NORA: (with no glance at Orrie): He's not Archie Goodwin. I knew Archie Goodwin the minute I saw him, Monday afternoon. I keep a scrapbook, Mr. Wolfe, a personal scrapbook. Among the things I put in it are pictures of people who have done things that I admire. There are three pictures of you, two from newspapers and one from a magazine, put in at different times, and one of Archie Goodwin. It was in the *Gazette* last year when you caught that murderer—you remember—Patrick Degan. I knew him the minute I saw him, and after I looked in my scrapbook there was no question about it.

(Orrie was looking straight at the pretty picture of the waterfall, at me though he couldn't see me, with blood in his eye, and

124

I couldn't blame him. He had been given to understand that the part was a cinch, that he wouldn't have to do or say anything to avert suspicion because she wouldn't have any. And there he was, a monkey. I couldn't blame him.)

WOLFE: (not visibly fazed, but also a monkey): I am flattered, Miss Kent, to be in your scrapbook. No doubt Mr. Goodwin is also flattered, though he might challenge your taste in having three pictures of me and only one of him. It will save—

NORA: Why did you send him there?

WOLFE: If you please. It will save time, and also breath, to proceed on an assumption, without prejudice. Obviously you're convinced that Mr. Goodwin took a job as Mr. Jarrell's secretary, and that I sent him, and it would be futile to try to talk you out of it. So we'll assume you're right. I don't concede it, but I'm willing to assume it for the sake of discussion. What about it?

NORA: I *am* right! You know it!

WOLFE: No. You may have it as an assumption, but not as a fact. What difference does it make? Let's get on. Did Mr. Goodwin take a job under his own name?

NORA: Certainly not. You know he didn't.

Mr. Jarrell introduced him to me as Alan Green.

WOLFE: Did you tell Mr. Jarrell that that wasn't his real name? That you recognized him as Archie Goodwin?

NORA: No.

WOLFE: Why not?

NORA: Because I wasn't sure what the situation was. I thought that Mr. Jarrell might have hired you to do something and he knew who Green was, but he didn't want me to know or anyone else. I thought in that case I had better keep it to myself. But now it's different. Now I think that someone else may have hired you, someone who wanted to know something about Mr. Jarrell's affairs, and you arranged somehow for Goodwin to take that job, and Mr. Jarrell doesn't know who he is.

WOLFE: You didn't have to come to me to settle that. Ask Mr. Jarrell. Have you?

NORA: No. I told you why. And then— there are reasons . . .

WOLFE: There often are. If none are at hand we contrive some. A moment ago you said, "But now it's different." What changed it?

NORA: You know what changed it. Mur-

126

der. The murder of Jim Eber. Archie Goodwin has told you all about it.

WOLFE: I'm willing to include that in the assumption. I think, madam, you had better tell me why you came here and what you want—still, of course, on our assumption.

(I said Monday afternoon that she didn't look her age, forty-seven. She did now. Her gray eyes were just as sharp and competent, and she kept her shoulders just as straight, but she seemed to have creases and wrinkles I hadn't observed before. Of course it could have been the light angle, or possibly it was looking through the waterfall.)

NORA: If we're assuming that I'm right, that man (indicating Orrie) can't be Archie Goodwin, and I don't know who he is. I haven't got *his* picture in my scrapbook. I'll tell *you* why I came.

WOLFE: That's reasonable, certainly. Archie, I'm afraid you'll have to leave us.

(Poor Orrie. As Orrie Cather he had been chased twice, and now he was chased as Archie Goodwin. His only hope now was to be cast as Nero Wolfe. When he was out and the door shut Nora spoke.)

NORA: All right, I'll tell you. Right after lunch today I went on an errand, and when I got back Mr. Jarrell told me the bullet

127

that killed Jim Eber was a thirty-eight. That was all he told me, just that. But I knew why he told me, it was because his own gun is a thirty-eight. He has always kept it in a drawer of his desk. I saw it there Wednesday afternoon. But it wasn't there Thursday morning, yesterday, and it hasn't been there since. Mr. Jarrell hasn't asked me about it, he hasn't mentioned it. I don't know—

WOLFE: Haven't you mentioned it?

(Orrie was at my elbow.)

NORA: No. If I mentioned it, and he had taken it himself, he would think I was prying into matters that don't concern me. I don't know whether he took it himself or not. But yesterday afternoon a man from Horland's Protective Agency delivered some pictures that must have been taken by the camera that works automatically when the door of the library is opened. The clock above the door said sixteen minutes past six. The pictures showed the door opening and a rug coming in—just the rug, flat, held up perpendicular, hanging straight down. Of course there was someone behind it. Archie Goodwin looked at the pictures, and of course he has told you all about it.

WOLFE: On our assumption, yes.

NORA: The camera must have taken them

the day before, at sixteen minutes past six Wednesday afternoon. At that hour I am always up in my room, washing and changing, getting ready to go to the lounge for cocktails. So is everyone else, nearly always. So there it is, take it altogether. On Monday Archie Goodwin comes as the new secretary under another name. Thursday morning Mr. Jarrell's gun is gone. Thursday afternoon the pictures come, taken at a time when I was up in my room alone. Friday morning, today, the news comes that Jim Eber has been murdered, shot. Also this morning Archie Goodwin isn't there, and Mr. Jarrell says he has sent him on a trip. And this afternoon Mr. Jarrell tells me that Jim was shot with a thirty-eight.

(The gray eyes were steady and cold. I had the feeling that if they aimed my way they would see me right through the picture, though I knew they couldn't.)

NORA: I'm not frightened, Mr. Wolfe. I don't scare easily. And I know you wouldn't deliberately conspire to have me accused of murder, and neither would Archie Goodwin. But all those things together, I wasn't going to just wait and see what happened. It wouldn't have helped any to say all this to Mr. Jarrell. I know all about his business affairs, but this is his personal life, his family, and I don't count. I'd rather not have him know I came to you, but I don't really care. I've worked long enough anyhow. Was Archie Goodwin there because Mr. Jarrell hired you, or was it someone else?

WOLFE: Even granting the assumption, I can't tell you that.

NORA: I suppose not. But he's not here today, so you may be through. In the twenty-two years I have been with Mr. Jarrell I have had many opportunities, especially the past ten years, and my net worth today, personally, is something over a million dollars. I know you charge high fees, but I could afford it. I said I'm not frightened, and I'm not, but something is going to happen to somebody, I'm sure of that, and I don't want it to happen to me. I want you to see that it doesn't. I'll pay you a retainer, of course, whatever you say. I believe the phrase is "to protect my interests."

WOLFE: I'm sorry, Miss Kent, but I must decline.

NORA: Why?

WOLFE: I've undertaken a job for Mr. Jarrell. He has—

NORA: Then he did hire you! Then he knew it was Archie Goodwin!

WOLFE: No. That remains only an assumption. He has engaged me to conduct a conference for him. On the telephone today. He feels that the situation calls for an experienced investigator, and at six o'clock, three hours from now, he will come here and bring seven people with him—his family, and a man named Brigham, and you. That is, if you care to come. Evidently you are in no mood to trot when he whistles.

NORA: He phoned you today?

WOLFE: Yes.

NORA: You were already working for him. You sent Archie Goodwin up there.

WOLFE: You have a right, madam, to your beliefs, but I beg you not to be tiresome with them. If you join us at six o'clock, and I advise you to, you should know that the Mr. Goodwin who scurried from this room at your behest will be here, at his desk, and Alan Green, Mr. Jarrell's secretary, will also be present. The others, the other members of Mr. Jarrell's family, unlike you, will probably be satisfied that those two men know who they are. Will you gain anything by raising the question?

NORA: No. I see. No. But I don't—then Mr. Jarrell doesn't know either?

WOLFE: Don't get tangled in your own

131

assumption. If you wish to revise it after the conference by all means do so. And now I ask you to reciprocate. I have an assumption too. We have accepted yours as a basis for discussion; now let us accept mine. Mine is that none of the people who will be present at the conference fired the shot that killed Mr. Eber. What do you think of it?

(The gray eyes narrowed.)

NORA: You can't expect me to discuss that. I am employed by Mr. Jarrell.

WOLFE: Then we'll turn it around. We'll assume the contrary and take them in turn. Start with Mr. Jarrell himself. He took his own gun, with that hocus-pocus, and shot Mr. Eber with it. What do you say to that?

NORA: I don't say anything.

(She stood up.)

NORA: I know you're a clever man, Mr. Wolfe. That's why your picture is in my scrapbook. I may not be as clever as you are, but I'm not an utter fool.

(She started off, and, halfway to the door, turned.)

NORA: I'll be here at six o'clock if Mr. Jarrell tells me to.

She went. I whispered to Orrie, "Go let her out, Archie." He whispered back, "Let her out yourself, Alan." The result was that

132

she let herself out. When I heard the front door close I left the wing and made it to the front in time to see her, through the one-way glass panel, going down the stoop. When she had reached the sidewalk safely I went to the office.

Wolfe was forward in his chair, his palms on his desk. Orrie was at my desk, in my chair, at ease. I stood and looked down at Wolfe.

"First," I said, "Who is whom?"

He grunted. "Confound that woman. When you were introduced to her Monday afternoon I suppose you were looking at her. And you saw no sign that she had recognized you?"

"No, sir. A woman who has it in her to collar a million bucks knows how to hide her feelings. Besides, I thought it was only women under thirty who put my pictures in scrapbooks. Then the program will be as scheduled?"

"Yes. Have you a reason for changing it?"

"No, sir. You're in for it. Please excuse me a minute." I pivoted to Orrie. "You'll be me at six o'clock, I can't help that, but you're not me now."

Down went my hands, like twin snakes

striking, and I had his ankles. With a healthy jerk he was out of my chair, and I kept him coming, and going, until he was flat on his back on the rug, six feet away. By the time he had bounced up I was sitting. I may not know how to deal with a murderer, but I know how to handle an imposter.

8

I made a crack, I remember, about Susan's entrance in the lounge Monday evening, after everyone else was there, as to whether or not she had planned it that way. My own entrance in Wolfe's office that Friday afternoon, after everyone else was there, was planned that way all right. There were two reasons: first, I didn't want to have to chat with the first arrivals, whoever they would be, while waiting for the others; and second, I didn't want to see Orrie being Archie Goodwin as he let them in and escorted them to the office. So at five-forty, leaving the furnishing of the refreshment table to Fritz and Orrie, I left the house and went across the street to the tailor shop, from where there was a good view of our stoop.

The first to show were Lois and Nora

Kent and Roger Foote, in a taxi. Nora paid the hackie, which was only fair since she could afford it, and anyway, she probably put it on the expense account. Transportation to and from a conference to discuss whether anyone present is a murderer is probably tax deductible. The next customer was also in a taxi—Corey Brigham, alone. Then came Wyman and Susan in a yellow Jaguar, with him driving. He had to go nearly to Tenth Avenue to find a place to park, and they walked back. Then came a wait. It was 6:10 when a black Rolls-Royce town car rolled to the curb and Jarrell and Trella got out. I hadn't grown impatient, having myself waited for Trella twenty-five minutes on Tuesday, bound for lunch at Rusterman's. As soon as they were inside I crossed the street and pushed the button. Archie Goodwin let me in and steered me to the office. He was passable.

He had followed instructions on seating. The bad thing about it was that I had four of them in profile and couldn't see the other's faces at all, but we couldn't very well give the secretary a seat of honor confronting the audience. Of course Jarrell had the red leather chair, and in the front row of yellow chairs were Lois, Trella, Wyman, and Susan. The family. Behind them were Alan Green, Roger Foote, Nora Kent, and Corey Brigham. At least I had Lois right in front of me. She wasn't as eye-catching from the back as from the front, but it was pleasant.

When Wolfe entered he accepted Jarrell's offer of a hand, got behind his desk, stood while Jarrell pronounced our names, inclined his head an eighth of an inch, and sat.

Jarrell spoke. "They all know that this is about Eber, and I've hired you, and that's all. I've told them it's a conference, a family conference, and it's off the record."

"Then I should clarify it." Wolfe cleared his throat. "If by 'off the record' you mean that I am pledged to divulge nothing that is said, I must dissent. I'm not a lawyer and cannot receive a privileged communication. If you mean that this proceeding is confidential and none of it will be disclosed except under constraint of law, if it ever applies, that's correct."

"Don't shuffle, Wolfe. I'm your client."

"Only if we understand each other." Wolfe's eyes went left to right and back again. "Then that's understood. I believe none of you know about the disappearance of Mr. Jarrell's gun. You have to know

136

that. Since his secretary, Mr. Green, was present when its absence was discovered, I'll ask him to tell you. Mr. Green?"

I had known that would come, but not that he would pick on me first. Their heads were turned to me. Lois twisted clear around in her chair, and her face was only arm's length away. I reported. Not as I had reported to Wolfe, no dialogue, but all the main action, from the time Jarrell had dashed into my room until we left the library. I had their faces.

The face that left me first was Trella's. She turned it to her husband and protested. "You might have told us, Otis!"

Corey Brigham asked me, "Has the gun been found?" Then he went to Jarrell too. "Has it?"

Wolfe took over. "No, it has not been found. It has not been looked for. In my opinion Mr. Jarrell should have had a search made at once, calling in the police if necessary, but it must be allowed that it was a difficult situation for him. By the way, Mr. Green, did you get the impression that Mr. Jarrell suspected anyone in particular?"

I hoped I got him right. Since he asked it he wanted it answered, but he hadn't asked what Jarrell had said, only if I had got an impression. I gave him what I thought he wanted. "Yes, I did. I might have been wrong, but I had the feeling that he thought he knew who had taken it. It was—"

"Goddamn it," Jarrell blurted, "you knew what I thought! I didn't think, I knew! If it's out let it come all the way out!" He aimed a finger at Susan. "You took it!"

Dead silence. They didn't look at Susan, they looked at him, all except Roger Foote, next to me. He kept his eyes on Wolfe, possibly deciding whether to place a bet on him.

The silence was broken by Wyman. He didn't blurt, he merely said, "That won't get you anywhere, Dad, not unless you've got proof. Have you got any?" He turned, feeling Susan's hand on his arm, and told her, "Take it easy, Sue." He was adding something, but Wolfe's voice drowned it.

"That point should be settled, Mr. Jarrell. Do you have any proof?"

"No. Proof for you, no. I don't need any."

"Then you'd better confine your charge to the family circle. Broadcast, it would be actionable." His head turned to the others. "We'll ignore Mr. Jarrell's specification of the culprit, since he has no proof. Ignoring that, this is the situation: When Mr. Jarrell learned this afternoon that Mr. Eber had been killed with a gun of the same caliber as his, which had been taken from a drawer of his desk, he was concerned, and no wonder, since Eber had been in his employ five years, had lived in his house, had recently been discharged, had visited his house on Wednesday, the day the gun was taken, and had been killed the next day. He decided to consult me. I told him that his position was precarious and possibly perilous; that his safest course was to report the disappearance of his gun, with all the circumstances, to the police; that, with a murder investigation under way, it was sure to transpire eventually, unless the murderer was soon discovered elsewhere; and that, now that I knew about it, I would myself have to report it, for my own protection, if the possibility that his gun had been used became a probability. Obviously, the best way out would be to establish that it was not his gun that killed Eber, and that can easily be done."

"How?" Brigham demanded.

"With an if, Mr. Brigham, or two of them. It can be established if it is true, and if the gun is available. Barring the servants, one of you took Mr. Jarrell's gun. Surrender it. Tell me where to find it. I'll fire a bullet from it, and I'll arrange for that bullet to be compared with the one that killed Eber. That will settle it. If the markings on the bullets don't match, the gun is innocent and I have no information for the police. Per contra, if they do match, I must inform the police immediately, and give them the gun, and all of you are in a pickle." He upturned both palms. "It's that simple."

Jarrell snapped at his daughter-in-law, "Where is it, Susan?"

"No," Wolfe snapped back at him, "that won't do. You have admitted you have no proof. I am conducting this conference at your request, and I won't have you bungling it. These people, including you, are jointly in jeopardy, at least of severe harassment, and I insist on making the appeal to them jointly." His eyes went right and left. "I appeal to all of you. Mrs. Wyman Jarrell." Pause. "Mr. Wyman Jarrell." Pause. "Mrs. Otis Jarrell." Pause. "Miss Jarrell." Pause. "Mr. Green." Pause. "Mr. Foote." Pause. "Miss Kent." Pause. "Mr. Brigham."

Lois twisted around in her chair to face me. "He's good at remembering names, isn't he?" she asked. Then she made two words,

140

four syllables, with her lips, without sound. I am not an accomplished lip reader, but there was no mistaking that. The words were "Archie Goodwin."

I was arranging my face to indicate that I hadn't caught it when Corey Brigham spoke. "I don't quite see why I have been included." His well-trained smile was on display. "It's an honor, naturally, to be considered in the Jarrell family circle, but as a candidate for taking Jarrell's gun I'm afraid I don't qualify."

"You were there, Mr. Brigham. Perhaps I haven't made it clear, or Mr. Green didn't. The photograph, taken automatically when the door opened, showed the clock above the door at sixteen minutes past six. You were a dinner guest that evening, Wednesday, and you arrived shortly after six and were in the lounge."

"I see." The smile stayed on. "And I rushed back to the library and worked the great rug trick. How did I get in?"

"Presumably, with a key. The door was intact."

"I have no key to the library."

Wolfe nodded. "Possession of a key to that room would be one of the many points to be explored in a laborious and prolonged inquiry, if it should come to that. Meanwhile you cannot be slighted. You're all on equal terms, if we ignore Mr. Jarrell's specification without evidence, and I do."

Roger Foote's voice boomed suddenly, louder than necessary. "I've got a question." There were little spots of color beneath the cheekbones of his big wide face—at least there was one on the side I could see. "What about this new secretary, this Alan Green? We don't know anything about him, anyway I don't. Do you? Did he know Eber?"

My pal. My pet panhandler. I had lent the big bum sixty bucks, my money as far as he knew, and this was what I got for it. Of course, Peach Fuzz hadn't won. He added a footnote. "He had a key to the library, didn't he?"

"Yes, Mr. Foote, he did," Wolfe conceded. "I don't know much about him and may have to know more before this matter is settled. One thing I do know, he says he was in his room alone at a quarter past six Wednesday afternoon, when the gun was taken. So was Mr. Jarrell, by his account. Mr. Green has told you of Mr. Jarrell's coming for him, and what followed. Mr. Brigham was in the lounge. Where were you, Mr. Foote?"

"Where was I when?"

"I thought I had made it plain. At a quarter past six Wednesday afternoon."

"I was on my back from Jamaica, and I got home—no. No, that was yesterday, Thursday. I must have been in my room, shaving. I always shave around then."

"You say 'must have been.' Were you?"

"Yes."

"Was anyone with you?"

"No. I'm not Louis the Fourteenth. I don't get an audience in to watch me shave."

Wolfe nodded. "That's out of fashion." His eyes went to Trella. "Mrs. Jarrell, we might as well get this covered. Do you remember where you were at that hour on Wednesday?"

"I know where I am at that hour every day—nearly every day, except week ends." I could see one of her ears, but not her face. "I was in the studio looking at television. At half past six I went to the lounge."

"You're sure you were there on Wednesday?"

"I certainly am."

"What time did you go to the studio?"

"A little before six. Five or ten minutes before."

"You remained there continuously until six-thirty?"

"Yes."

"I believe the studio is on the main corridor. Did you see anyone passing by in either direction?"

"No, the door was closed. And what do you take me for? Would I tell you if I had?"

"I don't know, madam; but unless we find that gun you may meet importunity that will make me a model of amenity by comparison." His eyes went past Wyman to Susan. "Mrs. Jarrell? If you please."

She replied at once, her voice down as usual, but firm and distinct. "I was in my room with my husband. We were together, from about a quarter to six, for about an hour. Then we went down to the lounge together."

"You confirm that, Mr. Jarrell?"

"I do." Wyman was emphatic.

"You're sure it was Wednesday?"

"I am."

Wolfe's eyes went left and were apparently straight at me, but I was on a line with Lois, who was just in front. "Miss Jarrell?"

"I think I'm it," she said. "I don't know exactly where I was at a quarter past six. I

144

was out, and I got home about six o'clock, and I wanted to ask my father something and went to the library, but the door was locked. Then I went to the kitchen to look for Mrs. Latham, but she wasn't there, and I found her in the dining room and asked her to iron a dress for me. I was tired and I started for the lounge to get a quick one, but I saw Mr. Brigham in there and I didn't feel like company, so I skipped it and went up to my room to change. If I had had a key to the library, and if I had thought of the rug stunt, I might have gone there in between and got the gun, but I didn't. Anyway, I hate guns. I think the rug was absolutely dreamy." She twisted around. "Don't you, Ar—Al—Alan?"

A marvelous girl. So playful. If I ever got her on a dance floor again I'd walk on her toes. She twisted back again when Wolfe asked a question.

"What time was it when you saw Mr. Brigham in the lounge? As near as you can make it."

She shook her head. "Not a chance. If it were someone I'm rather warm on, for instance Mr. Green, I'd say it was exactly sixteen minutes after six, and he would say he saw me looking in and he looked at his

145

watch, and we'd both be out of it, but I'm not warm on Mr. Brigham. So I won't even try to guess."

"This isn't a parlor game, Lois," her father snapped. "This may be serious."

"It already is, Dad. It sounds darned serious to me. You notice I told him all I could. Didn't I, Mr. Wolfe?"

"Yes, Miss Jarrell. Thank you. Will you oblige us, Miss Kent"

I was wondering if Nora would rip it. Not that it would have been fatal, but if she had announced that the new secretary was Archie Goodwin, that Wolfe was a damn liar when he gave them to understand that he had had no finger in the Jarrell pie until that afternoon, and that therefore they had better start the questions going the other way, it would have made things a little complicated.

She didn't. Speaking as a competent and loyal stenographer, she merely said, "On Wednesday Mr. Jarrell and I left the library together at six o'clock, as usual, locking the door. We took the elevator upstairs together and parted in the hall. I went to my room to wash and change, and stayed there until half past six, or a minute or two before that, perhaps twenty-eight minutes after six, and then I went down to the lounge."

Wolfe leaned back, clasped his fingers at the highest point of his central mound, took in a bushel of air and let it out, and grumbled, "I may have gone about this wrong. Of course one of you has lied."

"You're damn right," Jarrell said, "and I know which one."

"If Susan lied," Roger objected, "so did Wyman. What about this Green?"

I would walk on his toes too, some day when I could get around to it.

"It was a mistake," Wolfe declared, "to get you all on record regarding your whereabouts at that hour. Now you are all committed, including the one who took the gun, and he will be more reluctant than ever to speak. It would be pointless to hammer at you now; indeed, I doubt if hammering would have helped in any case. The time for hammering was Wednesday afternoon, the moment Mr. Jarrell found that the gun was gone. Then there had been no murder, with its menace of an inexorable inquisition."

He looked them over. "So here we are. You know how it stands. I said that I shall have to inform the police if the possibility that Mr. Jarrell's gun was used to kill Mr.

Eber becomes a probability. It is nearer a probability, in my mind, now than it was an hour ago—now that all of you have denied taking the gun, for one of you did take it."

His eyes went over them again. "When I speak to a man, or a woman, I like to look at him, but I speak now to the one who took the gun, and I can't look at him because I don't know who he is. So, speaking to him, I close my eyes." He closed them. "If you know where the gun is, and it is innocent, all you have to do is let it reappear. You need not expose yourself. Merely put it somewhere in sight, where it will soon be seen. If it does not appear soon I shall be compelled to make one of two assumptions."

He raised a finger, his eyes still closed. "One. That it is no longer in your possession and it is not accessible. If it left your possession before Eber was killed it may have been used to kill him, and the police will have to be informed. If it left your possession after he was killed and you know it wasn't used to kill him—and, as I said, that can be demonstrated—you will then have to expose yourself, but that will be a trifle since it will establish the innocence of the gun. I don't suppose Mr. Jarrell will prosecute for theft."

Another finger went up. "Two. My alternative assumption will be that you killed Eber. In that case you certainly will not produce the gun even if it is still available to you; and every hour that I delay telling the police what I know is a disservice to the law you and I live under."

He opened his eyes. "There it is, ladies and gentlemen. As you see it, it is exigent. There is nothing more to say at the moment. I shall await notice that the gun has been found, the sooner the better. The conference is ended, except for one of you. Mr. Foote suggested that the record of the man who took Mr. Eber's place, Mr. Alan Green, should be looked into, and I agree. Mr. Green, you will please remain. For the rest of you, that is all for the present. I should apologize for a default in hospitality. That refreshment table is equipped and I should have invited you. I do so now. Archie?"

Orrie Archie Cather Goodwin said, "I asked them, Mr. Wolfe," and got up and headed for the table. Roger Foote was there as soon as he was, so the bourbon would get a ride. Thinking it might be expected that my nerves needed a bracer, since my record was going to be probed, I went and asked Mr. Goodwin for some scotch and water.

The others had left their chairs, but apparently not for refreshment. Jarrell and Trella were standing at Wolfe's desk, conversing with him, and Corey Brigham stood behind them, kibitzing. Nora Kent stood at the end of the couch, sending her sharp gray eyes around. Seeing that Wyman and Susan were going, I caught Orrie's eye and he made for the hall to let them out. I took a sip of refreshment, stepped over to Roger Foote, and told him, "Many thanks for the plug."

"Nothing personal. It just occurred to me. What do I know about you? Nothing. Neither does anybody else." He went to the table and reached for the bourbon bottle.

I had been considering whether I should tackle Lois or let bad enough alone, and was saved the trouble when she called to me and I went to her, over by the big globe.

"We pretend we're looking at the globe," she said. "That's called covering. I just wanted to tell you that the minute I saw that character, when he let us in, I remembered. One thing I've got to ask, does my faher know who you are?"

She was pointing at Venezuela on the globe, and I was looking at her hand, which I knew was nice to hold to music. Obviously there was no chance of bulling it; she knew; and there wasn't time to take Wolfe's line with Nora and set it up as an assumption. So I turned the globe and pointed to Madagascar.

"Yes," I said, "he knows."

"Because," she said, "he may not be the flower of knighthood, but he's my father, and besides, he pays my bills. You wouldn't string me, would you?"

"I'd love to string you, but not on this. Your father knew I was Archie Goodwin when he took me to his place Monday afternoon. When he wants you and the others to know I suppose he'll tell you."

"He never tells me anything." She pointed to Ceylon. "If there was anything I wanted to blackmail you for, this would be wonderful, but if I ever do yearn for anything from you I would want it to pour out, just gush out from an uncontrollable passion. I wouldn't meet you halfway, because that wouldn't be maidenly, but I wouldn't run. It's too bad—"

"You coming, Lois?"

It was Roger Foote, with Nora beside him. Lois said the globe was the biggest one she had ever seen and she hated to leave it, and Roger said he would buy her one, what with I don't know, and they went. I stayed with the globe. Jarrell and Trella were still with Wolfe, but Corey Brigham had gone. Then they left too, ignoring me, and while Orrie was in the hall seeing them out I went and sat on one of the yellow chairs, the one Susan had occupied.

I cringed. "Very well, sir," I said, "you want my record. I was born in the maternity ward of the Ohio State Penitentiary on Christmas Eve, Eighteen sixty-five. After they branded me I was taken—"

"Shut up."

"Yes, sir." I got up and went to my own chair as Orrie appeared. "Do you want my opinion?"

"No."

"You're quite welcome. One will get you twenty that the gun will not be found."

He grunted.

I replied, "Lois has remembered who I am, and I had to tell her that her father knows. She won't spread it. One will get you thirty that the gun will not be found."

He grunted.

I replied, "To be practical about it, the only real question is how soon we call Cramer, and I'm involved in that as much as you are. More. One will get you fifty that the gun will not be found."

He grunted.

—9—

AT nine-thirty Saturday morning, having breakfasted with Lois and Susan and Wyman, more or less—more or less, because we hadn't synchronized—I made a tour of the lower floor of the duplex, all except the library and the kitchen. It wasn't a search; I didn't look under cushions or in drawers. Wolfe's suggestion had been to put the gun at some spot where it would soon be seen, so I just covered the territory and used my eyes. I certainly didn't expect to see it, having offered odds of fifty to one, and so wasn't disappointed.

There was no good reason why I shouldn't have slept in my own bed Friday night, but Wolfe had told Jarrell (with Trella there) that he would send his secretary back to him as soon as he was through asking him about his past. I hadn't really minded, since even a fifty-to-one shot has been known to deliver, and if one of them sneaked the gun out into the open that very evening it would be a pleasure to be the one to discover it, or even to be there when someone else discovered it. So I made a tour before I went to bed.

My second tour, Saturday morning, was more thorough, and when, having completed it, I entered the reception hall on my way to the front door, Steck was there.

He spoke. "Could I help you, sir? Were you looking for something?"

I regarded him. What if he was a loyal and devoted old retainer? What if he had been afraid his master was in a state of mind where he might plug somebody, and had pinched the gun to remove temptation? Should I take him up to my room for a confidential talk? Should I take him down to Wolfe? It would make a horse laugh if we unloaded to Cramer, and our client and his family were put through the wringer, and it turned out that the gun had been under Steck's mattress all the time. I regarded him, decided it would have to be referred to a genius like Wolfe, and told him I was beyond help, I was just fidgety, but thanked him all the same. When he saw I was going out he opened the door for me, trying not to look relieved.

Whenever possible I go out every morning some time between nine and eleven, when Wolfe is up in the plant rooms, to loosen up my legs and get a lungful of exhaust fumes, but it wasn't just through force of habit that I was headed outdoors. An assistant district attorney, probably accompanied by a dick, was coming to see Jarrell at eleven o'clock, to get more facts about James L. Eber, deceased, and Jarrell and I had agreed that it was just as well for me to be off the premises.

Walking the thirty blocks to the *Gazette* building, I dropped in to ask Lon Cohen if the Giants were going to move to San Francisco. I also asked him for the latest dope on the Eber murder, and he asked me who Wolfe's client was. Neither of us got much satisfaction. As far as he knew, the cops were making a strenuous effort to turn up a lead and serve the cause of justice, and as far as I knew, Wolfe was fresh out of clients but if and when I had anything good enough for the front page I would let him know. From there, having loosened up my legs, I took a taxi to 35th Street.

Wolfe had come down from the plant rooms and was at his desk, dictating to Orrie, at my desk. They took time out to greet me, which I appreciated, from two busy men with important matters to attend to like writing to Lewis Hewitt to tell him

155

that a cross of Cochlioda noezliana with Odontoglossum armainvillierense was going to bloom and inviting him to come and look at it. Not having had my usual forty minutes with the morning *Times* at breakfast, I got it from the rack and went to the couch, and had finished the front-page headlines and the sports pages when the doorbell rang. The man seated at my desk should have answered it, but he was being told by Wolfe how to spell a word which should have been no problem, so I went.

One glance through the panel, at a husky specimen in a gray suit, a pair of broad shoulders, and a big red face, was sufficient. I went and put the chain bolt on, opened the door to the two inches allowed by the chain, and spoke through the crack. "Good morning, I haven't seen you for months. You're looking fine."

"Come on, Goodwin, open up."

"I'd like to, but you know how it is. Mr. Wolfe is engaged, teaching a man how to spell. What do I tell him?"

"Tell him I want to know why he changed your name to Alan Green and got you a job as secretary to Otis Jarrell."

"I've been wondering about that myself. Make yourself comfortable while I go ask him. Of course if he doesn't know, there's no point in your bothering to come in."

Leaving the door open to the chain, not to be rude, I went to the office and crossed to Wolfe's desk. "Sorry to interrupt, but Inspector Cramer wants to know why you changed my name to Alan Green and got me a job as secretary to Otis Jarrell. Shall I tell him?"

He scowled at me. "How did he find out? That Jarrell girl?"

"No. I don't know. If you have to blame it on a woman, take Nora Kent, but I doubt it."

"Confound it. Bring him in."

I returned to the front, removed the chain, and swung the door open. "He's delighted that you've come. So am I."

He may not have caught the last three words, as he had tossed his hat on the bench and was halfway down the hall. By the time I had closed the door and made it back to the office, he was at the red leather chair. Orrie wasn't visible. He hadn't come to the hall, so Wolfe must have sent him to the front room. That door was closed. I went to my chair and was myself again.

Cramer, seated, was speaking. "Do you want me to repeat it? What I told Goodwin?"

"That shouldn't be necessary," Wolfe, having swiveled to face him, was civil but not soapy. "But I am curious, naturally, as to how you got the information. Has Mr. Goodwin been under surveillance?"

"No, but a certain address on Fifth Avenue has been, since eight o'clock this morning. When Goodwin was seen coming out, at a quarter to ten, and recognized, and it was learned from the man in the lobby that the man who had just gone out was named Alan Green and he was Otis Jarrell's secretary, and it was reported to me, I wasn't just curious. If I had been curious I would have had Sergeant Stebbins phone you. I've come myself."

"I commend your zeal, Mr. Cramer. And it's pleasant to see you again, but I'm afraid my wits are a little dull this morning. You must bear with me. I didn't know that taking a job under an alias is an offense against society and therefore a proper subject for police inquiry. And by you? The head of the Homicide Squad?"

"I ought to be able to bear with you, I've had enough practice. But by God, it's just about all I—" He stopped abruptly, got a cigar from a pocket, rolled it between his palms, stuck it in his mouth, and clamped his teeth on it. He never lit one. The mere sight of Wolfe, and the sound of his voice, with the memories they recalled, had stirred his blood, and it needed calming down.

He took the cigar from his mouth. "You're bad enough," he said, under control, "when you're not sarcastic. When you are, you're the hardest man to take in my jurisdiction. Do you know that a man named Eber was shot, murdered, in his apartment on Forty-ninth Street Thursday afternoon? Day before yesterday?"

"Yes, I know that."

"Do you know that for five years he had been Otis Jarrell's secretary and had recently been fired?"

"Yes, I know that too. Permit me to comment that this seems a little silly. I read the newspapers."

"Okay, but it's in the picture, and you want the picture. According to information received, Goodwin's first appearance at Jarrell's place was on Monday afternoon, three days before Eber was killed. Jarrell told the man in the lobby that his name was Alan Green and that he was going to live there. And he has been. Living there." His head jerked to me. "That right, Goodwin?"

"Right," I admitted.

"You've been there since Monday, under an assumed name as Jarrell's secretary?"

"Right—with time out for errands. I'm not there now."

"You're damn right you're not. You're not there now because you knew someone was coming from the DA's office to see Jarrell and you didn't want to be around. Right?"

"Fifth Amendment."

"Nuts. That's for Reds and racketeers, not for clowns like you." He jerked back to Wolfe, decided his blood needed calming again, stuck the cigar in his mouth, and chewed on it.

He removed it. "That's the picture, Wolfe," he said. "We've got no lead that's worth a damn on who killed Eber. Naturally our best source on his background and his associates has been Jarrell and the others at his place. Eber not only worked there, he lived there. We've got a lot of facts about him, but nothing with a motive for murder good enough to fasten on. We're just about ready to decide we're not going to get anywhere with Jarrell and that bunch and we'd better concentrate on other possibilities, and then this. Goodwin. Goodwin and you."

His eyes narrowed, then he realized that

was the wrong attitude and opened them. "Now it's different. If a man like Otis Jarrell hires you for something so important that you're even willing to get along without Goodwin so he can go and stay under an assumed name, with a job as Jarrell's secretary, and if the man who formerly had the job gets murdered three days later, do you expect me to believe there's no connection?"

"I'm not sure I follow you, Mr. Cramer. Connection between what?"

"Like hell you don't follow me! Between whatever Jarrell hired you for and the murder!"

Wolfe nodded. "I assumed you meant that, but I am wary of assumptions. You should be too. You are assuming that Mr. Jarrell hired me. Have you grounds for that? Isn't it possible that someone else hired me, and I imposed Mr. Goodwin on Mr. Jarrell's household to get information for my client?"

That settled it. Ever since I had opened the door a crack and got Cramer's message for Wolfe, I had been thinking that Wolfe would probably decide that the cat was too scratchy to hang onto, and would let Cramer take it, but not now. Jarrell's gun would not be mentioned. The temptation to teach

Cramer to be wary of assumptions had been irresistible.

Cramer was staring. "By God," he said. "Who's your client? No. I'd never pry that out of you. But you can tell me this: was Eber your client?"

"No, sir."

"Then is it Jarrell or isn't it? Is Jarrell your client?"

Wolfe was having a picnic. "Mr. Cramer. I am aware that if I have information relevant to the crime you're investigating I am bound to give it to you; but its relevance may be established, not by your whim or conjecture, but by an acceptable process of reason. Since you don't know what information I have, and I do, you can't apply that process and it must be left to me. My conclusion is that I have nothing to tell you. I have answered your one question that was clearly relevant, whether Mr. Eber was my client. You will of course ask Mr. Jarrell if he is my client, telling him his secretary is my confidential assistant, Archie Goodwin; I can't prevent that. I'm sorry you gave yourself the trouble of coming, but your time hasn't been entirely wasted; you have learned that I wasn't working for Mr. Eber."

Cramer looked at me, probably because,

for one thing, if he had gone on looking at Wolfe he would have had to get his hands on him; and for another, there was the question whether I might possibly disagree with the conclusion Wolfe had reached through an acceptable process of reason. I met his look with a friendly grin which I hoped wouldn't strike him as sarcastic.

He put the cigar in his mouth and closed his teeth on it, got up, risked another look at Wolfe, not prolonged, turned, and tramped out. I stayed put long enough for him to make it down the hall, then went to see if he had been sore enough to try the old Finnegan on us. He hadn't; he was out, pulling the door shut as he went.

As I stepped back into the office Wolfe snapped at me, "Get Mr. Jarrell."

"The assistant DA is probably still with him."

"No matter, get him."

I went to my desk, dialed, got Nora Kent, and told her that Mr. Wolfe wished to speak to Mr. Jarrell. She said he was engaged and would call back and I said the sooner the better because it was urgent. Say two minutes. It wasn't much more than that before the ring came, and Jarrell was on, and Wolfe got at his phone. I stayed at mine.

Jarrell said he had gone to another phone because two men from the district attorney's office were with him, and Wolfe asked, "Have they mentioned Mr. Goodwin or me?"

"No, why should they?"

"They might have. Inspector Cramer of the Homicide Squad was here and just left. The entrance to your address is under surveillance and Mr. Goodwin was recognized when he came out this morning, and it has been learned that he has been there as your secretary since Monday, with Alan Green as his name. Mr. Goodwin told you what would happen if that were disclosed, and it has happened. I gave Mr. Cramer no information whatever except that Mr. Eber was not my client. Of course you—"

"Did you tell him what I hired you for?"

"You're not listening. I said I gave him no information whatever. I didn't even tell him that you hired me, let alone what for. Of course they'll be at you immediately, since they know about Mr. Goodwin. I suggest that you reflect on the situation with care. Whatever you tell them, do not fail to inform me at once. If you admit that you hired me—"

164

"What the hell, I've got to admit it! You say they know about Goodwin!"

"So they do. But I mentioned to Mr. Cramer the possibility that someone else hired me to send Goodwin there to spy on you. Merely as a possibility. Please understand that I told him nothing."

"I see." Silence. "I'll be damned." Silence. "I'll have to think it over and decide what to say."

"You will indeed. It will probably be best for you to tell them that you hired me on a personal and confidential matter, and leave it at that. But on one point, between you and me, there must be no ambiguity. I am free to disclose what I know about your gun, and its disappearance, at any moment that I think it necessary or desirable. You understand that."

"That's not the way you put it. You said you'd have to report it if the possibility that my gun was used to kill Eber became a probability."

"Yes, but the decision rests with me. I am risking embarrassment and so is Mr. Goodwin. We don't want to lose our licenses. It would have been prudent to tell Mr. Cramer when he was here, but he provoked me."

He hung up and glared at me as if I had done the provoking.

I hung up and glared back. "License my eye," I told him. "We're risking eating on the State of New York for one to ten years with time off for good behavior."

"Do you challenge me?" he demanded. "You were present. You have a tongue, heaven knows. Would you have loosened it if I hadn't been here?"

"No," I admitted. "He goes against the grain. He has bad manners. He lacks polish. Look at you for contrast. You are courteous, gracious, tactful, eager to please. What now? I left up there to be out of the way when company came, but now they're on to me. Do I go back?"

He said no, not until we heard further from Jarrell, and I went to the front room to tell Orrie to come and get on with the day's work, and then returned to the couch and the *Times*.

10

THE other day I looked up "moot" in the dictionary. The murderer of James L. Eber had just been convicted, and, discussing it,

Wolfe and I had got onto the question of whether or not a life would have been saved if he had told Cramer that Saturday morning about Jarrell's gun, and he had said it was moot, and, though I thought I knew the word well enough, I went to the dictionary to check. In spite of the fact that I had taken a position just to give the discussion some spirit, I had to agree with him on that. It was moot all right, and it still is.

The thirty hours from noon Saturday until six o'clock Sunday afternoon were not without events, since even a yawn is an event, but nobody seemed to be getting anywhere, least of all me. Soon after lunch Saturday, at Wolfe's table with him and Orrie, Jarrell phoned to tell us the score. Cramer had gone straight there from our place to join the gathering in the library. Presumably he hadn't started barking, since even an inspector doesn't bark at an Otis Jarrell unless he has to, but he had had questions to which he intended to get answers. Actually he had got only one answered: had Jarrell hired Nero Wolfe to do something? Yes. Plus its rider: had Archie Goodwin, alias Alan Green, come as Jarrell's secretary to do the something Wolfe had been hired for, or to help do it? Yes. That was all. Jarrell had told them that the something was a personal and confidential matter, with no bearing on their investigation, and that therefore they could forget it.

It was a cinch Cramer wouldn't forget it, but evidently he decided that for the present he might as well lump it, for there wasn't a peep out of him during those thirty hours.

I could see no point in Alan Green's getting back into the picture, and apparently Jarrell couldn't either, for he also reported that Alan Green was no more. He was telling the family, and also Corey Brigham, who I was and why, but was leaving the why vague. He had engaged the services of Nero Wolfe on a business matter, and Wolfe had sent me there to collect some facts he needed. He was also telling them I wouldn't be back, but on that Wolfe balked. I was going back, and I was staying until further notice. When Jarrell asked what for, Wolfe said to collect facts. When Jarrell asked what facts, Wolfe said facts that he needed. Jarrell, knowing that if I wasn't let in he would soon be letting Cramer in to ask about a gun, had to take it. When Wolfe had hung up and pushed his phone back I had asked him to give me a list of the facts he needed.

"How the devil can I," he demanded,

"when I don't know what they are? If something happens I want you there, and with you there it's more likely to happen. Now that they know who you are, you are a threat, a pinch at their nerves, at least for one of them, and he may be impelled to act."

Since it was May it might have been expected that at least some of them would be leaving town for what was left of the week end, and they probably would have if their nerves weren't being pinched. Perhaps Jarrell had told them to stick around; anyway, they were all at the dinner table Saturday. Their attitude toward me, with my own name back, varied. Roger Foote thought it was a hell of a good joke, his asking Wolfe to investigate my past; he couldn't get over it, and didn't. Trella not only couldn't see the joke; she couldn't see me. Her cooing days were over as far as I was concerned. Wyman didn't visibly react one way or another. Susan went out of her way to indicate that she still regarded me as human. In the lounge at cocktail time she actually came up to me as I was mixing a Bloody Mary for Lois, and said she hoped she wouldn't forget and call me Mr. Green.

"I'm afraid," she added, almost smiling,

"that my brain should have more cells. It put you and that name, Alan Green, in a cell together, and now it doesn't know what to do."

I told her it didn't matter what she called me as long as it began with G. I hadn't forgotten that she was supposed to be a snake, or that she had been the only one to bid me welcome, or that she had pulled me halfway across a room on an invisible string. That hadn't happened again, but once was enough. I didn't have her tagged yet, not by any means. As a matter of fact, I was a little surprised to see her and Wyman still there, since Jarrell had accused her of swiping his gun before witnesses. Maybe, I thought, they were staying on just to get that detail settled. Her little mouth in her little oval face could have found it hard to smile, not because it was shy but because it was stubborn.

I had supposed there would be bridge after dinner, but no. Jarrell and Trella had tickets for a show, and Wyman and Susan for another show. Nora Kent was going out, destination unspecified. Roger Foote suggested gin for an hour or so, saying that he had to turn in early because he was going to get up at six in the morning to go to

Belmont. I asked what for, since there was no racing on Sunday, and he said he had to go and look at the horses. Declining his gin invitation, I approached Lois. There was no point in my staying in for the evening, since there would be no one there to have their nerves pinched except Roger, and he was soon going to bed, so I told Lois that now that my name was changed it would be both possible and agreeable to take her to the Flamingo Club. She may have had no plans because her week end had been upset, or she may have had plans but took pity on me, or my charm may simply have been too much for her. Anyhow, we went, and got home around two o'clock.

On Sunday it looked at first as if I might do fairly well as a threat. Four of them were at breakfast with me—Wyman, Susan, Lois, and Nora. Jarrell had already had his and gone out somewhere, Roger had gone to look at horses, and I gathered that Trella wasn't up yet. But the future didn't look promising. Nora was going to church and then to the Picasso show at the Modern Museum, apparently to spend the day. Susan was going to church. Wyman went to the side terrace with an armload of Sunday papers. So when Lois said she was going for a walk I said I was too and which way should I head, away from her or with her? She said we could try with and see how it worked. I found that she wouldn't walk in the park, probably on acount of squirrels, so we kept to the avenues, Madison and Park. After half an hour she took a taxi to go to have lunch with friends, not named. I was invited to come along, but thought I had better go and see if there was anyone around to be threatened. On the way back I phoned Wolfe to tell him what had happened: nothing. In the reception hall, Steck told me Jarrell wanted me in the library.

He thought he had news, but I wasn't impressed. He had spent an hour at the Penguin Club with an old friend, or at least an old acquaintance, Police Commissioner Kelly, and had been assured that while the district attorney and the police would do their utmost to bring the murderer of Jarrell's former secretary to the bar of justice, there would be no officious prying into Jarrell's private affairs. Respectable citizens deserved to be treated with respect, and would be. Jarrell said he was going to ring Wolfe to tell him about it, and I said that would be fine. I didn't add that Wolfe would be even less impressed than I was. Officious prying would be no name for it if and when they learned about Jarrell's gun.

Having bought a newspaper of my own on the way back, I went to the lounge with it, finding no one there, and caught up with the world, including the latest non-news on the Eber murder. There was no mention of the startling fact that Otis Jarrell's new secretary had turned out to be no other than Nero Wolfe's man Friday, Saturday, Sunday, Monday, Tuesday, Wednesday, and Thursday, the celebrated detective, Archie Goodwin. Evidently Cramer and the DA weren't going to give us any free publicity until and unless we were involved in murder, a typical small-minded attitude of small men, and it was up to Wolfe's public-relations department, namely me, to do something about it; and besides, I owed Lon Cohen a bone. So I went up to my room and phoned him, and wished I hadn't, since he tried to insist on a hunk of meat with it. I had no sooner hung up than a ring called me to the green phone. It was Assistant District Attorney Mandelbaum, who invited me to appear at his office at three o'clock that afternoon for a little informal chat. I told him I would be delighted, and went down to get some oats, having been informed by Steck that lunch would be at one-thirty.

Lunch wasn't very gay, since there were only three of them there—Jarrell, Wyman, and Susan. Susan said maybe three words altogether, as for instance, "Will you have cream, Mr. Goodwin?" When I announced that I would have to leave at two-thirty for an appointment at the district attorney's office, thinking it might pinch a nerve, Wyman merely used a thumb and forefinger to pinch his thin straight nose, whether or not meant as a vulgar insult I couldn't say, and Susan merely said that she supposed talking with an assistant district attorney was nothing for a detective but she would be frightened out of her wits. Jarrell said nothing then, but when we left the table he took me aside and wanted to know. I told him that since the police commissioner had promised that there would be no officious prying into his private affairs there was no problem. I would just tell Mandelbaum that I was part of Mr. Jarrell's private affairs and therefore a clam.

Which I did. Having stopped on the way to phone Wolfe because he always likes to know where I am, I was a little late, arriving in the anteroom at 3:02 p.m., and then I was kept waiting exactly one hour and seventeen minutes. Taken into Mandelbaum at 4:19, I was in no mood to tell him anything whatever except that he was a little balder and a little plumper than when I had last seen him, but he surprised me. I had expected him to try to bulldoze me, or sugar me, into spilling something about my assignment at Jarrell's, but he didn't touch on that at all. Apparently Jarrell's session with the commissioner had had some effect. After apologizing for keeping me waiting, Mandelbaum wanted to know what I had seen and heard when I entered the studio at noon on Wednesday and found James L. Eber there with Mrs. Wyman Jarrell. Also whether I had seen Eber with anyone else or had heard anyone say anything about him.

Since that was about Eber and his movements and contacts the day before he was killed, I couldn't very well say that I concluded by an acceptable process of reasoning that it was irrelevant, so I obliged. I even gave him verbatim the words that had passed among Eber and Susan and me. He spent some time trying to get me to remember other words, comments that had been made in my hearing about Eber and his appearance there that day, but on that I passed. I had heard a few, chiefly at the lunch table, and had reported them to Wolfe, but none of them had indicated any desire or intention to kill him, and I saw no point in supplying them for the record.

It was for the record. A stenographer was present, and after Mandelbaum finished with me I had another wait while a statement was typed for me to sign. Reading it, I could find nothing that needed changing, so I signed it "Archie Goodwin, alias Alan Green." I thought that might as well be on record too.

Back at my threatening base at twenty minutes to six, I found that bridge was under way in the lounge, but only one table: Jarrell, Trella, Wyman, and Nora. Steck informed me, when asked, that neither Lois nor Roger had returned, and that Mrs. Wyman Jarrell was in the studio. Proceeding down the corridor and finding the studio door open, I entered.

The only light was from the corridor and the television screen. Susan was in the same chair as before, in the same spot. Since she was concentrating on the screen, with the discussion panel, "We're Asking You," it wasn't much of a setup from a professional standpoint, but personally it might be interesting. The conditions were precisely the same as formerly, and I wanted to see. If I felt another trance coming on I could make a dash for the door and safety. Not to cut her view of the screen, I circled behind her chair and took the one on the other side.

I would have liked to look at her, her profile, instead of the screen, giving her magic every chance, but she might have misunderstood, so I kept my eyes on "We're Asking You" clear to the end. I didn't learn much. They were asking what to do about extra-bright children, and since I didn't have any and intended to stay as far away as I could from those I had seen and heard on TV and in the movies, I wasn't concerned.

When they got it settled and the commercial started Susan turned to me. "Shall I leave it on for the news?"

"Sure, might as well, I haven't heard the baseball scores."

I never did hear them, not on that TV set. It was Bill Brundage, the one who has the trick of rolling his eyes up, pretending he's looking for a word, when it's right there in front of him and everybody knows it. I listened with one ear while he gave us the latest on the budget, Secretary Dulles, a couple of Senatorial investigations, and so forth, and then suddenly he got both ears.

"The body of Corey Brigham, well-known socialite and man-about-town, was found this afternoon in a car parked on Thirty-ninth Street near Seventh Avenue. According to the police, he had been shot in the chest. The body was on the floor of the car in front of the rear seat, covered with a rug. It was discovered when a boy saw the toe of a shoe at the edge of the rug and notified a policeman. The windows of the car were closed and there was no gun in the car. Mr. Corey Brigham lived at the Churchill Towers. He was a bachelor and was a familiar figure in society circles and in the amusement world."

Susan's fingers had gripped my arm, with more muscle than I would have guessed she had. Apparently just realizing it, she took her hand back and said, "I beg your pardon." Her voice was low, as always, and Bill Brundage was talking, but I caught it, and that's what she said. I reached across her lap to the chair on the other side and flipped the switch on the control box.

"Corey Brigham?" she said. "He said Corey Brigham, didn't he?"

"He certainly did." I got up, went to the

door, turned on lights, and came back. "I'm going to tell Mr. Jarrell. Do you want to come?"

"What?" Her face tilted up. It was shocked. "Oh, of course, tell them. You tell them."

Evidently she wasn't coming, so I left her. Going along the corridor I was thinking that the news might not be news to one of them. It was even possible that it hadn't been news to Susan. At the card table in the lounge they were in the middle of a hand, and I went and stood until the last trick was raked in.

"I wasted my queen, damn it," Jarrell said. He turned to me. "Anything new, Goodwin?"

"Not from the district attorney," I told him. "Just routine, about the last time I saw Jim Eber—and for me the only time. Now he'll be asking about the last time I saw Corey Brigham. You too. All of you."

I had three of their faces: Jarrell, Trella and Wyman. Nora was shuffling. None of them told me anything. There was no point in prolonging it, so I went on. "Something new on TV just now. The body of Corey Brigham has been found in a parked car. Shot. Murdered."

Jarrell said, "Good God. No!" Nora stopped shuffling and her head jerked to me. Trella's blue eyes stretched at me. Wyman said, "You wouldn't be pulling a gag, would you?"

"No gag. Your wife was there, I mean in the studio. She heard it."

Wyman shoved his chair back and was up and gone. Jarrell demanded, "Found in a car? Whose car?"

"I don't know. For what I do know I'll give you the broadcast verbatim. I'm good at that." I did so, not trying to copy Bill Brundage's delivery, just his words. At the end I added, "Now you know all I know."

Trella spoke. "You said he was murdered. That didn't say murder. He might have shot himself."

I shook my head. "No gun in the car."

"Anyway," Nora said, "he wouldn't have got under a rug. If Corey Brigham was going to shoot himself he would do it in the dining room of the Penguin Club." It wasn't meant as it reads; she was merely stating a fact.

"He had no family," Trella said. "I guess we were his closest friends. Shouldn't we do something, Otis?"

"You don't need me," I said. "I'm sorry

I had to break up your game." To Jarrell: "I'll be with Mr. Wolfe, in case."

"No." He was emphatic. "I want you here."

"You'll soon be too busy to bother with me. First your former secretary, and now your friend Brigham. I'm afraid that calls for officious prying, and I'd rather not be in the way."

I moved, and I didn't mosey. I was surprised that someone hadn't already come, since they had got sufficently interested in the Jarrells to collect miscellaneous facts and collection must have included the name of Corey Brigham. The one who came might be Lieutenant Rowcliff—it was his kind of errand; and while I liked nothing better than twisting Rowcliff's ear, I wasn't in the humor for it at the moment. I wanted a word with Wolfe before twisting anyone's ear, even Rowcliff's. So I didn't mosey, leaving the premises, crossing the avenue, and getting a taxi headed downtown.

When I entered the office Wolfe was there alone, no Orrie on Sunday, and one glance at him was enough. He had a book in his hand, with a finger inserted to keep his place, but he wasn't reading, and a good caption for a picture of the face he turned to me would have been *The Gathering Storm*.

"So," I said, crossing to his desk, "I see I don't bring news. You've already heard it."

"I have," he growled. "Where were you?"

"Watching television with Susan. We heard it together. I notified Jarrell and his wife and Wyman and Nora Kent. Lois and Roger Foote weren't there. Nobody screamed. Then I beat it to come and get instructions. If I had stayed I wouldn't have known whether the time has come to let the cat out or not. Do you?"

"No."

"Do you mean you don't know or the time hasn't come?"

"Both."

I swiveled my chair around and sat. "That's impossible. If I said a thing like that you'd say I had a screw loose, only you never use that expression. I'll put it in simplest terms. Do you wish to speak to Cramer?"

"No. I'll speak to Mr. Cramer only when it is requisite." The gathering storm had cleared some. "Archie. I'm glad you came. I confess I needed you, to say no to. Now that I have said it, I can read." He opened the book. "I will speak to no one on the phone, and no one will enter my door, until I have more facts." His eyes went to the book and he was reading.

I was glad he was glad I had come, but I wasn't glad, if I make myself clear. I might as well have stayed up there and twisted Rowcliff's ear.

—11—

I slept in my own bed that night for the first time in nearly a week.

That was a very interesting period, Sunday evening and part of Monday. I suppose I noticed what Wolfe said, that he would see no one and hear no one until he had more facts. Exactly how he thought he would get facts, under the conditions he imposed, seeing or hearing no one, I couldn't say. Maybe by ESP or holding a séance. However, by noon on Monday it had become evident that he hadn't meant it that way. What he had really meant was that he wanted no facts. If he had seen a fact coming he would have shut his eyes, and if he had heard one coming he would have stuck fingers in his ears.

So it was a very interesting period. There

he was, a practicing private detective with no other source of income except selling a few orchid plants now and then, with a retainer of ten grand in cash in the safe, with a multi-millionaire client with a bad itch, with a fine fat fee in prospect if he got a move on and did some first-class detecting; and he was afraid to stay in the same room with me for fear I would tell him something. He wouldn't talk with Jarrell on the phone. He wouldn't turn on the radio or television. I even suspected that he didn't read the *Times* Monday morning, though I can't swear to that because he reads the *Times* at breakfast, which is taken up to his room by Fritz on a tray. He was a human ostrich with his head stuck in the sand, in spite of the fact that he resembles an ostrich in physique less than any other human I know of with the possible exception of Jackie Gleason.

All there was to it, he was in a panic. He was scared stiff that any minute a fact might come bouncing in that would force him to send me down to Cramer bearing gifts, and there was practically nothing on earth he wouldn't rather do, even eating ice cream with cantaloupe or putting horseradish on oysters.

I understood how he felt, and I even sympathized with him. On the phone with Jarrell, both Sunday evening and Monday morning, I did my best to string him along, telling him that Wolfe was sitting tight, which he was, God knows, and explaining why it was better for me to be out of the way, at least temporarily. It wasn't too bad. Lieutenant Rowcliff had called on the Jarrell family, as I had expected, but hadn't been too nasty about the coincidence that two of Jarrell's associates, his former secretary and a close friend, had got it within a week. He had been nasty, of course—Rowcliff would be nasty to Saint Peter if he ever got near him; but he hadn't actually snarled.

But although I sympathized with Wolfe, I'm not a genius like him, and if I was sliding into a hole too deep to crawl out of I wanted to know about it in time to get a haircut and have my pants pressed before my appearance in the line-up. Of the half a dozen possible facts that could send me over the edge there was one in particular that I wanted very much to get a line on, but it wasn't around. None of the newscasts mentioned it, Sunday night or Monday morning. It wasn't in the Monday morning papers. Lon Cohen didn't have it. There were four guys—one at headquarters, one on the DA's staff, and two on Homicide—for whom I had done favors in the past, who could have had it and who might have obliged me, but with two murders in the stew it was too risky to ask them.

So I was still factless when, ten minutes before noon, the phone rang and I got an invitation to call at the DA's office at my earliest convenience. Wolfe was still up in the plant rooms. He always came down at eleven o'clock, but hadn't shown that morning—for fear, as I said, that I would tell him something. I buzzed him on the house phone to tell him where I was going, went out and walked to Ninth Avenue, and took a taxi to Leonard Street.

That time I was kept waiting only a few minutes before I was taken in to Mandelbaum. He was polite, as usual, getting to his feet to shake hands. I was only a private detective, true, but as far as he knew I had committed neither a felony nor a misdemeanor, and the only way an assistant DA can get the "assistant" removed from his title is to have it voted off, making it DA, and I was a voter. The chair for me at the end of his desk was of course placed so I was facing a window.

What he wanted from me was the same as before, things I had seen and heard at Jarrell's place, but this time concentrating on Corey Brigham instead of James L. Eber. I had to concede that that had now become relevant, and there was more ground to cover since Brigham had been there for dinner and bridge on Monday, and again on Wednesday, and also I might have heard comments about him at other times. Mandelbaum was patient, and thorough, and didn't try to be tricky. He did double back a lot, but doubling back has been routine for so many centuries that you can't call it a trick. I didn't mention one of my contacts with Brigham, the conference at Wolfe's office Friday afternoon, and to my surprise he didn't either. I would have thought they would have dug that up by now, but apparently not.

After he told the stenographer to go and type the statement, and she went, I stood up. "It will take her quite a while," I said. "I have to run a couple of errands, and I'll drop in later and sign it. If you don't mind."

"Quite all right. Certainly. If you make it today. Say by five o'clock."

"Oh, sure." I turned to go, and turned back, and grinned at him. "By the way, you may have noticed that I didn't live up to my reputation for wisecracks."

"Yes, I noticed that. Maybe you're running out."

"I hope not. I'll do better the next time. I guess my mind was too busy with something I had just heard—about the bullets."

"What bullets?"

"Why, the two bullets. Haven't you got that yet? That the bullet that killed Eber and the one that killed Brigham were fired by the same gun?"

"I thought that was—" He stopped. "Where did you hear that?"

I gave him another grin. "I know, it's being saved. Don't worry, I won't slip it out—I may not even tell Mr. Wolfe. But it won't keep long, it's too hot. The guy who told me, it was burning his tongue, and he knows me."

"Who was it? Who told you?"

"I *think* it was Commissioner Kelly. There's a wisecrack, I seem to be recovering. I suppose I shouldn't have mentioned it. Sorry. I'll be in to sign the statement before five." I was going. He called after me, wanting to know who had told me, but I said I couldn't remember, and went.

So the fact was a fact, and I had it. I

hadn't risked anything. If it had turned out not to be a fact, and his reaction would have shown it, it could have been that someone had been stringing me, and of course I wouldn't have remembered who. Okay, I had it. If Wolfe had known what I was bringing home with me he would probably have locked himself in his room and not answered the phone, and I would have had to yell through the door.

He had just sat down to lunch—red snapper filets baked in butter and lemon juice and almonds—so I had to hold it. Even without the rule that business was taboo at the table, I wouldn't have had the heart to ruin his meal. But I still might want time to get a haircut and have my pants pressed, so as soon as we had crossed to the office and coffee had been poured I spoke. "I hate to bring it up right after lunch, but I think you ought to know. We're out of the frying pan. We're in the fire. At least that is my opinion."

He usually takes three little sips of coffee at its hottest before putting the cup down, but that time, knowing my tones of voice, he took only two.

"Opinion?"

"Yes, sir. It may be only that because it's

an inference. For more than an hour Mandelbaum asked me what I had seen and heard from, by, to, and about Corey Brigham. I said I'd drop in later to sign the statement, got up to go, and said something. So you can form your own opinion, I'll give it to you."

I did so. His frown at the start was a double-breasted scowl at the end. He said nothing, he just scowled. It isn't often that his feelings are too strong for words.

"If you want to," I said, "you can be sore at me for fishing it up. If I hadn't worked that on him it would have been another day, possibly two, before you had to face it. But you can be sore and use your mind at the same time, I've seen you, and it looks to me as if a mind is needed. I'm assuming that your opinion is the same as mine."

He snorted. "Opinion? Bah. He might as well have certified it."

"Yes, sir."

"He's a simpleton. He should have known you were gulling him."

"Yes, sir. You can be sore at him."

"Soreness won't help. Nor will it help to use my mind—supposing that I have one. This is disaster. There is only one forlorn issue to raise: whether we should verify it before we act, and if so how."

"If you had been there I doubt if you would think it was necessary. If you could have seen his face when he said 'I thought that was—' and chopped it off."

"No doubt. He's a simpleton."

He flattened his palms on his desk and stared into space. That didn't look promising. It didn't seem he was using his mind; when he uses his mind he leans back and closes his eyes, and when he's hard at it his lips go in and out. So he wasn't working. He was merely getting set to swallow a pill that would taste bad even after it was down and dissolved. It took him a full three minutes.

Then he transferred his palms to the chair arms and spoke. "Very well. Your notebook. A letter to Mr. Jarrell, to be delivered at once by messenger. It might be best to take it yourself, to make sure he gets it without delay."

He took a breath. "Dear Mr. Jarrell. I enclose herewith my check for ten thousand dollars, returning the retainer you paid me in that amount for which I gave you a receipt. My outlay for expenses has not been large and I shall not bill you.

"Paragraph. A circumstance has transpired which makes it necessary for me to report to the proper authority some of the information I have acquired while acting on your behalf, particularly the disappearance of your Bowdoin thirty-eight revolver. Not being at liberty to specify the circumstance, I will say only that it compels me to take this step in spite of my strong inclination against it. I shall take it later this afternoon, after you have received this letter and the enclosure.

"Paragraph. I assume, naturally, that in this situation you will no longer desire my services and that our association ceases forthwith. In the unlikely event that you—"

He stopped short and I raised my eyes from the notebook. His lips were clamped tight and a muscle at the side of his neck was twitching. He was having a fit.

"No," he said. "I will not. Tear it up."

I hadn't cared much for it myself. I put the pen down, ripped the two pages from the notebook, tore them across three times, and dropped them in the wastebasket.

"Get Mr. Cramer," he said.

I cared for that even less. Apparently he had decided it was too ticklish to wait even a few hours and was going to let go even

192

before notifying the client. Of course that wasn't unethical, with two murders sizzling, but it was rather unindomitable. I would have liked to take a stand, but in the first place he was in no mood for one of my stands, and in the second place the only alternative was the letter to Jarrell and that had been torn up. So I got Cramer, who, judging from his tone, was in a mood too. He told Wolfe he could give him a minute.

"That may do," Wolfe said. "You may remember our conversation Saturday. Day before yesterday."

"Yeah, I remember it. What about it?"

"I said then that if I have reason to think I have information relevant to the crime you're investigating I am bound to give it to you. I now suspect that I have such information but I want to make sure. To do so I must proceed on the basis of knowledge that has come to to me in a peculiar manner and I don't know if I can rely on it. Mr. Goodwin has learned, or thinks he has, that the markings on the bullet which killed Corey Brigham have been compared with those on the bullet which killed James L. Eber, and that they are identical. I can proceed to verify my suspicion only if I accept that as established, and I decided to consult you. Do you advise me to proceed?"

"By God," Cramer said.

"I'm afraid," Wolfe objected, "that I need something more explicit."

"Go to hell and get it there," Cramer advised. "I know where Goodwin got it, from that damn fool at Leonard Street. He wanted us to find out who had leaked it to Goodwin, and we wanted to know exactly what Goodwin had said, and he told us, and we told him if he wanted to know who leaked it to Goodwin just look in a mirror. And now you've got the gall to ask me to verify it. By God. If you've got relevant information about a murder you know where it belongs."

"I do indeed. And I'll soon know whether I have it or not if I proceed on the basis of Mr. Goodwin's news. If and when I have it you'll get it without undue delay. Do you advise me to proceed?"

"Look, Wolfe. Are you listening?"

"Yes, I'm listening."

"Okay, you want my advice. Here it is. Get the written permission of the police commissioner and the mayor too, and then proceed all you want to."

He hung up.

I did too, and swiveled, and spoke. "So that's settled. It was the same gun. And in spite of it, Jarrell's private affairs are still private, or we'd be downtown right now, both of us, and wouldn't get home for dinner. By the way, I apologize. I thought you were going to cough it up."

"I am, confound it. I'll have to. But not until I get the satisfaction of a gesture. Get Mr. Jarrell."

"Where he can talk?"

"Yes."

That took a little doing. Nora Kent answered and said he was on the other phone, long distance, and also someone was with him, and I told her to have him call Wolfe for a private conversation as soon as possible. While we waited Wolfe looked around for something to take his mind off his misery, settled on the big globe, and got up and walked over to it. Presumably he was picking a spot to head for, some remote island or one of the poles, if he decided to lam. When the phone rang and I told him it was Jarrell he took his time getting to it.

"Mr. Jarrell? I have in my hand a letter which Mr. Goodwin has just typed, dictated by me, which I intended to send you at once by messenger, but on second thought I'm going to read it to you first. Here it is."

He read it. My notes were in the wastebasket, but my memory is good too, and not a word was changed. It was just as he had dictated it. He even finished the last sentence, which he had left hanging: " 'In the unlikely event that you wish me to continue to act for you, let me know at once. Sincerely.' That's the letter. It occurs to me—"

"You can't do that! What's the circumstance?"

"No, sir. As I said in the letter, I'm not at liberty to reveal it, at least not in a letter, and certainly not on the telephone. But it occurs—"

"Get this straight, Wolfe. If you give anybody information about my private affairs that you got working for me in a confidential capacity, you'll be sorry for it as long as you live!"

"I'm already sorry. I'm sorry I ever saw you, Mr. Jarrell. Let me finish, please. It occurs to me that there is a chance, however slim, that a reason can be found for ignoring the circumstance. I doubt it, but I'm willing to try. When I dictated the letter I intended to ask Mr. Cramer to visit me here at six

196

o'clock, three hours from now. I'll postpone it on one condition, that you come at that hour and bring with you everyone who was here on Friday—except Mr. Brigham, who is dead—with the—"

"What for? What good will that do?"

"If you'll let me finish. With the understanding that you stay, all of you, until I am ready to adjourn, and that I will insist on answers to any questions I ask. I can't compel answers, but I can insist, and I may learn more from refusals to answer than from the answers I get. That's the condition. Will you come?"

"What do you want to ask about? They have already told you they didn't take my gun!"

"And you have told me that you know your daughter-in-law took it. Anyway, one of them lied, and I told them so. You'll know what I want to ask about when you hear me. Will you come?"

He balked for another five minutes, among other things demanding to know what the circumstance was that had made Wolfe write the letter, but only because he was used to being at the other end of the whip and it was a new experience for him. He had no choice and knew it.

Wolfe hung up, shook his head like a bull trying to chase a fly, and rang for beer.

—12—

WOLFE started it off with a bang. He surveyed them with the air of a judge about to impose a stiff one, and spoke, in a tone that was meant to be offensive and succeeded.

"There is nothing to be crafty about so I won't try. When you were here on Friday my main purpose was to learn which of you had taken Mr. Jarrell's gun; today it is to learn which of you used it to kill Mr. Eber and Mr. Brigham. I am convinced that one of you did. First I'll—Don't interrupt me!"

He glared at Jarrell, but it was more the voice than the glare that stopped Jarrell with only two words out. Wolfe doesn't often bellow, and almost never at anyone but Cramer or me, but when he does he means it. Having corked the client, who was in the red leather chair, he gave the others the glare. In front were Susan, Wyman, Trella, and Lois, as before. With Brigham no longer available and me back where I belonged, there were only two in the rear, Nora Kent and Roger Foote.

"I will not be interrupted." It was as positive as the bellow, though not so loud. "I have no more patience for you people—including you, Mr. Jarrell. Especially you. First I'll explain why I am convinced that one of you is a murderer. To do so I'll have to disclose a fact that the police have discovered but are keeping to themselves. If they learn that I've told you about it and are annoyed, then they'll be annoyed. I am past regard for trivialities. The fact is that the bullets that killed Eber and Brigham came from the same gun. That, Mr. Jarrell, is the circumstance I spoke of on the phone."

"How do—"

"Don't interrupt. The technical basis of the fact is of course a comparison of the bullets in the police laboratory. How I learned it is not material. So much for the fact; now for my conclusion from it. The bullets are thirty-eights; the gun that was taken from Mr. Jarrell's desk was a thirty-eight. On Friday I appealed to all of you to help me find Mr. Jarrell's gun, and told you how, if it was innocent, it could be recovered with no stigma for anyone. Surely, if it was innocent, one of you would have acted on that appeal, but you didn't, and it was therefore a permissible conjecture that the gun had been used to kill Eber, but only a conjecture. Now it is no longer a conjecture; it has reached the status of a reasonable assumption. For Brigham was killed by a bullet from the gun that killed Eber, and those two men were both closely associated with you people. Eber lived with you for five years, and Brigham was in your familiar circle. Not only that, they were both concerned in the matter which I was hired to investigate one week ago today, the matter which took Mr. Goodwin there—"

"That'll do! You know what—"

"Don't interrupt!" It was close to a bellow again. "The matter which took Mr. Goodwin there under another name. I need not unfold that matter; enough that it was both grave and exigent, and that both Eber and Brigham were involved in it. So consider a hypothesis: that those two men were killed by some outsider with his own private motive, and it is merely a chain of coincidences that they were both in your circle, that the gun was the same caliber as Mr. Jarrell's, that Mr. Jarrell's gun was taken by one of you the day before Eber was killed, and that in spite of my appeal the gun has not been found. If you can swallow that hypothesis, I can't. I reject it, and I conclude that one of you is a murderer. That is our starting point."

"Just a minute." It was Wyman. His thin nose looked thinner, and the deep creases in his brow looked deeper. "That may be your starting point, but it's not mine. Your man Goodwin here was there. What for? All this racket about a stolen gun—what if he took it? That's your kind of stunt, and his too, and of course my father was in on it. That's *my* starting point."

Wolfe didn't waste a bellow on him. He merely shook his head. "No, sir. Apparently you don't know what you're here for. You're here to give me a chance to wriggle out of a predicament. I am desperate. I dislike acting under compulsion in any case, and I abominate being obliged to divulge information about a client's affairs that I have received in confidence. The starting point is my conclusion that one of you is a murderer, not to go on from there to identify the culprit and expose him—that isn't what I was hired for—but to show you the fix I'm in. What I desperately need is not sanction for my conclusion, but plausible ground for rejecting it. I want to impeach it. As for your notion that Mr. Goodwin took the gun, in a stratagem devised by me with your father's knowledge, that is mere drivel and is no credit to your wit. If it had happened that way I would be in no predicament at all; I would produce the gun myself, demonstrate its innocence, and have a good night's sleep."

"If death ever slept," Lois blurted.

Their heads all turned to her. Not, probably, that they expected her to supply anything helpful; they were glad to have an excuse to take their eyes off Wolfe and relieve the strain. They hadn't been exchanging glances. Apparently no one felt like meeting other eyes.

"That's all," Lois said. "What are you all looking at me for? That just came out."

The heads went back to Wolfe. Trella asked, "Am I dumb? Or did you say you want us to prove you're wrong?"

"That's one way of putting it, Mrs. Jarrell. Yes."

"How do we prove it?"

Wolfe nodded. "That's the difficulty. I don't expect you to prove a negative. The simplest way would be to produce the gun, but I've abandoned hope of that. I don't intend to go through the dreary routine of inquiry on opportunity; that would take all night, and checking your answers would take an army a week, and I have no army. But I have gathered from the public reports that Eber died between two o'clock and six o'clock Thursday afternoon, and Brigham died between ten o'clock Sunday morning and three o'clock that afternoon, so it may be possible to exclude one or more of you. Has anyone an alibi for either of those periods?"

"You've stretched the periods," Roger Foote declared. "It's three to five Thursday and eleven to two Sunday."

"I gave the extremes, Mr. Foote. The extremes are the safest. You seem well informed."

"My God, I ought to be. The cops."

"No doubt. You'll soon see much more of them if we don't discredit my conclusion."

"You can start by excluding me," Otis Jarrell said. "Thursday afternoon I had business appointments, three of them and got home a little before six. Sunday—"

"Were the appointments all at the same place?"

"No. One downtown and two midtown. Sunday morning I was with the police commissioner at the Penguin Club for an hour, from ten-thirty to eleven-thirty, went straight home, was in my library until lunch time at one-thirty, returned to the library and was there until five o'clock. So you can exclude me."

"Pfui." Wolfe was disgusted. "You can't be as fatuous as you sound, Mr. Jarrell. Your Thursday is hopeless, and your Sunday isn't much better. Not only were you loose between the Penguin Club and your home, but what about the library? Were you alone there?"

"Most of the time, yes. But if I had gone out I would have been seen."

"Nonsense. Is there a rear entrance to your premises?"

"There's a service entrance."

"Then it isn't even worth discussing. A man with your talents and your money, resolved on murder, could certainly devise a way of getting down to the ground without exposure." Wolfe's head moved. "When I invited exclusion by alibis I didn't mean to court inanities. Can any of you furnish invulnerable proof that you must be eliminated for either of those periods?"

"On Sunday," Roger Foote said, "I went to Belmont to look at horses. I got there at nine o'clock and I didn't leave until after five."

"With company? Continuously?"

"No. I was always in sight of somebody, but a lot of different people."

"Then you're no better off than Mr. Jarrell. Does anyone else want to try, now that you know the requirements?"

Apparently nobody did. Wyman and Susan, who were holding hands, looked at each other but said nothing. Trella turned to look at her brother and muttered something I didn't catch. Lois just sat, and so did Jarrell.

Then Nora Kent spoke. "I want to say something, Mr. Wolfe."

"Go ahead, Miss Kent. You can't make it any worse."

"I'd like to make it better—for me. If you're making an exception of me you haven't said so, and I think you should. I think you should tell them that I came to see you Friday afternoon and what I said."

"You tell them. I'll listen."

But she kept focused on him. "I came right after lunch on Friday. I told you that I had recognized the new secretary as Archie Goodwin as soon as I saw him, and I asked why you had sent him, and whether Mr. Jarrell had hired you or someone else had. I told you that the murder of Jim Eber had made me think I had better try to find out what the situation was. I told you I had discovered that Mr. Jarrell's gun was missing from the drawer of his desk, and that I had just found out that the caliber of the bullet that killed Jim Eber was the same as Mr. Jarrell's gun. I told you that I wasn't frightened, but I didn't want to just wait and see what happened, and I wanted to hire you to protect my interests and pay you a retainer. Is that correct?"

"It is indeed, madam. And well reported. And?"

"And I wanted Mr. Jarrell to know. I wanted them all to know. And I wanted to be sure that you hadn't forgotten."

"You may be. And?"

"And I wanted it on the record. I don't think they're going to discredit your conclusion. I think you're going to tell the police about the gun, and I know what will happen then. I would appreciate it if you'll tell them that I came to see you Friday and what I said. I'll tell them myself, of course, but I wish you would. I'm not frightened, but—"

Jarrell had been controlling himself. Now he exploded. "Damn you, Nora! You saw

Wolfe Friday, three days ago? And didn't tell me?"

She sent the gray eyes at him. "Don't yell at me, Mr. Jarrell. I won't have you yelling at me, not even now. Will you tell the police, Mr. Wolfe?"

"I will if I see them, Miss Kent, and I agree with you, reluctantly, that I'm probably going to." He took in the audience. "There is a third period, a brief one, which I haven't mentioned, because we covered it on Friday—from six to six-thirty Wednesday afternoon, when the gun was taken. None of you was excluded from that, either, not even Mr. Brigham, but he is now." He went to Jarrell. "I bring that up, sir, because you stated explicitly that your daughter-in-law took the gun, but you admitted that you have no proof. Have you any now?"

"No. Proof that you would accept, no."

"Have you proof that anyone would accept?"

"Certainly he hasn't." It was Wyman. He was looking, not at Wolfe, but at his father. But he said, "he," not "you," though he was looking at him. "And now it's a little too much. Now it may not be just taking a gun, it may be killing two men with it. Of course he has no proof. He hates her, that's all. He wants to smear her. He made passes at her, he kept it up for a year, and she wouldn't let him touch her, and so he hates her. That's all there is to it."

Wolfe made a face. "Mrs. Jarrell. You heard what your husband said?"

Susan nodded, just perceptibly. "Yes, I heard."

"Is it true?"

"Yes. I don't want—" she closed her mouth and opened it again. "Yes, it's true."

Wolfe's head jerked left. "Mr. Jarrell. Did you make improper advances to your son's wife?"

"No!"

Wyman looked straight at his father and said distinctly, "You're a liar."

"Oh, my God," Trella said. "This is fine. This is wonderful."

If I know any man who doesn't need feeling sorry for it's Nero Wolfe, but I came close to it then. After all the trouble he had taken to get them there to help him out of his predicament, they had turned his office into a laundromat for washing dirty linen.

He turned and snapped at me, "Archie, draw a check to Mr. Jarrell for ten thousand dollars." As I got up and went to the safe for the checkbook he snapped at them, "Then it's hopeless. I was afraid it would be, but it was worth trying. I admit I made the effort chiefly for the sake of my own self-esteem, but also I felt that you deserved this last chance, at least some of you. Now you're all in for it, and one of you is doomed. Mr. Jarrell, you don't want me any more, and heaven knows I don't want you. Some of Mr. Goodwin's things are up there in the room he occupied, and he'll send or go for them. The check, Archie?"

I gave it to him, he signed it, and I went to hand it to Jarrell. I had to go to the far side of the red leather chair to keep from being bumped by Wolfe, who was on his way out and who needs plenty of room whether at rest or in motion. Jarrell was saying something, but Wolfe ignored it and kept going.

They left in a bunch, not a lively bunch. I accompanied them to the hall, and opened the door, but no one paid any attention to me except Lois, who offered a hand and frowned at me—not a hostile frown, but the kind you use instead of a smile when you are out of smiles for reasons beyond your control. I frowned back to show that there was no hard feeling as far as she was concerned.

I watched them down the stoop to the sidewalk through the one-way glass panel, and when I got back to the office Wolfe was there behind his desk. As I crossed to mine he growled at me, "Get Mr. Cramer."

"You're riled," I told him. "It might be a good idea to count to ten first."

"No. Get him."

I sat and dialed WA 9-8241, Manhattan Homicide West, asked for Inspector Cramer, and got Sergeant Purley Stebbins. He said Cramer was in conference downtown and not approachable. I asked how soon he would be, and Purley said he didn't know and what did I want.

Wolfe got impatient and picked up the receiver. "Mr. Stebbins? Nero Wolfe. Please tell Mr. Cramer that I shall greatly appreciate it if he will call on me this evening at half past nine—or, failing that, as soon as his convenience will permit. Tell him I have important information for him regarding the Eber and Brigham murders. . . . No, I'm sorry, but it must be Mr. Cramer. . . . I know you are, but if you come without Mr. Cramer you will not be admitted. With him you will be welcome. . . . As soon as he can make it, then."

As I hung up I spoke. "One thing, anyhow, there is no longer—"

I stopped because I had turned and seen that he had leaned back and shut his eyes, and his lips had started to go in and out. He was certainly desperate. It was only fifteen minutes until dinner time.

—13—

I would say that Inspector Cramer and Sergeant Stebbins weigh about the same, around one-ninety, and little or none of it is fat on either of them, so you would suppose their figures would pretty well match, but they don't. Cramer's flesh is tight-weave and Stebbins' is loose-weave. On Cramer's hands the skin follows the line of the bones, whereas on Stebbins' hands you have to take the bones for granted, and presumably they are like that all over, though I have never played with them on the beach and so can't swear to it. I'm not sure which of them would be the toughest to tangle with, but some day I may find out, even if they are officers of the law.

That was not the day, that Monday evening. They were there by invitation, to get a handout, and after greeting Wolfe and sitting—Cramer in the red leather chair and Purley near him, against the wall, on a yellow one—they wore expressions that were almost neighborly. Almost. Cramer even tried to be jovial. He asked Wolfe how he was making out with his acceptable process of reason.

"Not at all," Wolfe said. He had swiveled to face them and wasn't trying to look or sound cordial. "My reason has ceased to function. It has been swamped in a deluge of circumstance. My phone call, to tell you that I have information for you, was dictated not by reason but by misfortune. I am sunk and I am sour. I just returned a retainer of ten thousand dollars to a client. Otis Jarrell. I have no client."

You might have expected Cramer's green eyes to show a gleam of glee, but they didn't. He would swallow anything that Wolfe offered only after sending it to the laboratory for the works. "That's too bad," he rumbled. "Bad for you but good for me. I can always use information. About Eber and Brigham, you said."

Wolfe nodded. "I've had it for some time,

but it was only today, a few hours ago, that I was forced to acknowledge the obligation to disclose it. It concerns an event that occurred at Mr. Jarrell's home last Wednesday, witnessed by Mr. Goodwin, who reported it to me. Before I tell you about it I need answers to a question or two. I understand that you learned from Mr. Jarrell that he had hired me for a job, and that it was on that job that Mr. Goodwin went there as his secretary under another name. I also understand that he declines to tell you what the job was, on the ground that it was personal and confidential and has no relation to your inquiry; and that the police commissioner and the district attorney have accepted his position. That you have been obliged to concur is obvious, since you haven't been pestering Mr. Goodwin and me. Is that correct?"

"It's correct that I haven't been pestering you. The rest, what you understand, I can't help what you understand."

"But you don't challenge it. I understand that too. I only wanted to make it clear why I intend to tell you nothing about the job Mr. Jarrell hired me for, though he is no longer my client. I assume the police commissioner and the district attorney wouldn't want me to, and I don't care to offend them. Another question, before I—yes, Mr. Stebbins?"

Purley hadn't said a word. He had merely snarled a little. He set his jaw.

Wolfe resumed to Cramer. "Another question. It's possible that my piece of information is bootless because your attention is elsewhere. If so, I prefer not to disclose it. Have you arrested anyone for either murder?"

"No."

"Have you passable grounds for suspicion of anyone outside of the Jarrell family?"

"No."

"Now a multiple question which can be resolved into one. I need to know if any discovered fact, not published, renders my information pointless. Was someone, presumably the murderer, not yet identified, seen entering or leaving the building where Eber lived on Thursday afternoon? The same for Brigham. According to published accounts, it is assumed that someone was with him in the back seat of his car, which was parked at some spot not under observation, that the someone shot him, covered the body with a rug, drove the car to Thirty-ninth Street near Seventh Avenue, from where the subway was easily and quickly accessible, parked the car, and decamped. Is that still the assumption? Has anyone been found who saw the car, either en route or while being parked, and can describe the driver? To resolve them into one: Have you any promising basis for inquiry that has not been published?"

Cramer grunted. "You don't want much, do you? You'd better have something. The answer to the question is no. Now let's hear it."

"When I'm ready. I am merely taking every advisable precaution. My information carries the strong probability that the two murders were committed by Otis Jarrell, his wife, Wyman Jarrell, his wife, Lois Jarrell, Nora Kent, or Roger Foote. Or two or more of them in conspiracy. So another question. Do you know anything that removes any of those people from suspicion?"

"No." Cramer's eyes had narrowed. "So that's what it's like. No wonder you got from under. No wonder you gave him back his retainer. Let's have it."

"When I'm ready," Wolfe repeated. "I want something in return. I want a cushion for my chagrin. You will be more than satisfied with what I give you, and you will not begrudge me a crumb of satisfaction for myself. After I give you my information I want some from you. I want a complete report of the movements of the seven people I named, and I want the report to cover a considerable period: from two o'clock Thursday afternoon to three o'clock Sunday afternoon. I want to know everywhere they went, with an indication of what has been verified by your staff and what has not. I'm not asking for—"

"Save it," Cramer rasped. "You asking! You're in a hell of a position to ask. You've been withholding material evidence, and it's got too hot for you and you've got to let go. Okay, let go!"

He might not have spoken as far as Wolfe was concerned. He took up where he left off. "I'm not asking for much. You already have some of that and will now be getting the rest of it, and all you need to do is let Mr. Goodwin copy the reports of their movements. That will reveal no departmental secrets, and that's all I want. I'm not haggling. If you refuse my request you'll get what you came for anyway; I have no choice. I make the request in advance only because as soon as I give you the information you'll be leaving. You'll have urgent business and wouldn't wait to hear me. Will you oblige me?"

"I'll see. I'll consider it. Come on, spill it."

Wolfe turned to me. "Archie?"

Since I had been instructed I didn't have to ask him what to spill. I was to tell the truth, the whole truth, and nothing but the truth about the gun, and that was all. I did so, beginning with Jarrell dashing into my room at 6:20 Wednesday afternoon, and ending twenty-four hours later at Wolfe's office, with my report to him. When I finished Purley was on the edge of his chair, his jaw clamped, looking holes through me. Cramer was looking at Wolfe.

"Goddamn you," he said. "Four days. You've had this four days."

"Goodwin's had it five days," Purley said.

"Yeah." Cramer transferred to me. "Okay, go on."

I shook my head. "I'm through."

"Like hell you're through. You'll be surprised. If you—"

"Mr. Cramer," Wolfe cut in. "Now that you have it, use it. Railing at us won't help any. If you think a charge of obstructing justice will hold, get a warrant, but I advise against it. I think you'd regret it. As soon as the possibility became a probability I acted. And when it was merely a possibility I explored it. I had them all here, on Friday, including Mr. Brigham, and told them that the gun must be produced. Yesterday, when the news came about Brigham, it was touch and go. Today, when Mr. Goodwin learned about the bullets, it became highly probable, but I felt I owed my client at least the gesture, and I had them here again. It was fruitless. I repaid Mr. Jarrell's retainer, dismissed them, and phoned you. I will not be squawked at. I have endured enough. Either get a warrant, or forget me and go to work on it."

"Four days," Cramer said. "When I think what we've been doing those four days. What are you hanging onto? What else have you got? Which one was it?"

"No, sir. If I had known that I would have called you here, not to give it up but to deliver the murderer. I would have been exalted, not mortified. I haven't the slightest notion."

"It was Jarrell himself. It was Jarrell, and he was your client, and you cut him loose, but you wouldn't deliver him on account of your goddamn pride."

Wolfe turned. "Archie. How much cash is in the safe?"

"Thirty-seven hundred dollars in the reserve and around two hundred in petty."

"Bring me three thousand."

I went and opened the door of the safe, unlocked the cash drawer and opened it, counted three grand from the reserve stack, and stepped to Wolfe's desk and handed it to him. With it in his fist he faced Cramer.

"The wager is that when this is over and the facts are known you will acknowledge that at this hour, Monday evening, I had no inkling of the identity of the murderer, except that I had surmised that it was one of the seven people I have named, and I have told you that. Three thousand dollars to three dollars. One thousand to one. You have three dollars? Mr. Stebbins can hold the stakes."

Cramer looked at Stebbins. Purley grunted. Cramer looked at me. I grinned and said, "For God's sake grab it. A thousand to one? Give me that odds and I'll bet you I did it myself."

"That's not as funny as you think it is, Goodwin. You could have." Cramer looked at Wolfe. "You know I know you. You know I never yet saw you open a bag and shake it out without hanging onto a corner that had something in it you were saving for yourself. If you're backing clear out, if you've got no client and no fee in sight, why do you want the reports on their movements from two o'clock Thursday to three o'clock Sunday?"

"To exercise my brain." Wolfe put the stack of bills on the desk and put a paperweight—a chunk of jade that a woman had once used to crack her husband's skull—on top. "It needs it, heaven knows. As I said, I want a crumb of satisfaction for myself. Do you believe in words of honor?"

"I do when the honor is there."

"Am I a man of honor?"

Cramer's eyes widened. He was flabbergasted. He started to answer and stopped. He had to consider. "You may be, at that," he allowed. "You're tricky, you're foxy, you're the best liar I know, but if anybody asked me to name something you had done that was dishonorable I'd have to think."

"Very well, think."

"Skip it. Say you're a man of honor. What about it?"

"Regarding the reports I have asked for, to exercise my brain on. I give my word of honor that I have no knowledge, withheld from you, which can be applied to those reports; that when I inspect them I'll have no relevant facts that you don't have."

"That *sounds* good." Cramer stood up. "I was going home, and now this. I've heard you sound good before. Who's at my desk, Purley? Rowcliff?"

"Yes, sir." Stebbins was up too.

"Okay, let's get started. Come on, Goodwin, get your hat if you've got one big enough."

I knew that was coming. It would probably go on all night, and my style would be cramped because if they got exasperated Wolfe wouldn't get the reports to exercise his brain on. I didn't even remark that I didn't wear a hat when I went slumming.

14

THAT was twenty minutes past ten Monday night. At six o'clock Wednesday afternoon, when Wolfe came down from the plant rooms, I had just finished the last of the timetables and had them ready for him.

It had taken that long to fill his order, for three reasons. First, the city and county employees hadn't got started on the trails of the Jarrells until Tuesday morning, and each of the subjects was given two sittings before Cramer got the results. Second, Cramer didn't decide until Wednesday noon that he would let Wolfe have it, though I had known darned well he would, since it included nothing he wanted to save, and since he was curious to see what Wolfe wanted with it. And third, after I had been given permission to look at a selected collection of the reports, it took quite a job of digging to get what Wolfe wanted, not to mention my own contributions and the typing after I got home.

I can't tell you what Wolfe did Tuesday and Wednesday because I wasn't there to see, but if you assume that he did nothing whatever I won't argue—that is, nothing but eat, sleep, read, drink beer, and play with orchids. As for me, I was busy. Monday night they kept me at 20th Street—Rowcliff and a Sergeant Coffey—until four o'clock in the morning, going over it back and forth and across and up and down, and when they got through they knew every bit as much as Cramer and Stebbins had already known when they took me down. Rowcliff could not believe that he wasn't smart enough to maneuver me into leaking what I was at Jarrell's for, and I didn't dare to make it clear to him in words he would understand for fear he might see to it that Wolfe didn't get what he wanted for brain exercise. So daylight was trying to break through at my windows when I turned in.

And Tuesday at noon, when I had just started on my fourth griddle cake and my second cup of coffee, the phone rang to tell me that I would be welcome at the DA's office in twenty minutes. I made it in forty, and was there five solid hours, one of them with the DA himself present, and at the end they knew everything that Rowcliff did. There was one little spot where the chances looked good for my getting booked as a material witness, but I bumped through it without having to yell for help.

My intention was, if and when I left Leonard Street a free man, to stop in at Homicide West to see if Cramer had decided to let me look at the reports, but I was interrupted. After finally being dismissed by Mandelbaum, as I was on my way down the hall from his room to the front, a door on the right opened and one of the three best dancers I had ever stepped with came out. Seeing me, she stopped.

"Oh," she said. "Hello."

An assistant DA named Riley, having opened the door for her, was there shutting it. He saw me, thought he would say something, decided not to, and closed the door. The look Lois was giving me was not an invitation to dance, far from it.

"So," she said, "you've made it nice for us, you and your fat boss."

"Then don't speak to me," I told her. "Give me an icy stare and flounce out. As for making it nice for you, wrong address. We held on till the last possible tenth of a second."

"Hooray for you. Our hero." We were moving down the hall. "Where are you bound for?"

"Home, with a stopover."

We were in the anteroom, with people there on chairs. She waited until we were in the outer hall to say, "I think I want to ask you something. If we go where we can get a drink, by the time we get there I'll know."

I looked at my wrist. Ten minutes to six. We no longer had a client to be billed for expenses, but there was a chance she would contribute something useful for the time-tables, and besides, looking at her was a pleasant change after the five hours I had just spent. So I said I'd be glad to buy her a drink whether she decided to ask me something or not.

I took her to Mohan's, which was in walking distance around the corner, found an empty booth at the far end, and ordered. When the drinks came she took a sip of her Bloody Mary, made a face, took a bigger sip, and put the glass down.

"I've decided to ask you," she said. "I ought to wait until I've had a couple because my nerves have gone back on me. When I saw you there in the hall my knees were shaking."

"After you saw me or before?"

"They were already shaking. I knew I'd have to tell about it, I knew that yesterday, but I was afraid nobody would believe me. That's what I want to ask you, I want you to back me up and then they'll have to believe me. You see, I know that nobody used my father's gun to kill Jim Eber and Corey Brigham. I want you to say you were with me when I threw it in the river."

I raised my brows. "That's quite a want. God knows what you might have wanted if you waited till you had a couple. You threw your father's gun in the river?"

"Yes." She was making her eyes meet mine. "Yes, I did."

"When?"

"Thursday morning. That's how I know nobody could have used it, because Jim was killed Thursday afternoon. I got it the day before, Wednesday, you know how I got it, going in with that rug held up in front of me. I hid it—"

"How did you open the library door?"

"I had a key. Jim Eber let me have a duplicate made from his—about a year ago. Jim was rather warm on me for a while. I hid the gun in my room, under the mattress. Then I was afraid Dad might have the whole place searched and it would be found, so I got rid of it. Don't you want to know why I took it?"

"Sure, that would help."

"I took it because I was afraid something might happen. I knew how Dad felt about Susan, and I knew it was getting worse every day between him and Wyman, and I knew he had a gun in his drawer, and I hate guns anyway. I didn't think any one thing— I didn't think he would shoot Susan or Wyman would shoot him—I just thought something might happen. So Thursday morning I put it in my bag and went and got my car, and drove up the West Side Highway and onto George Washington

Bridge, and stopped on the bridge and threw the gun in the river."

She finished the drink and put the glass down. "Naturally I never intended to tell anybody. Friday morning, when the news came that Jim Eber had been shot, it never occurred to me that that had anything to do with Dad's gun. How could it, when I knew Dad's gun was in the river? Then that afternoon at Nero Wolfe's office I saw how wrong I was. What he suggested, that whoever took the gun should put it out in sight somewhere, naturally I would have done that if I could—but I was afraid that if I told what I had done no one would believe me. It would sound like I was just trying to explain it away. Could I have a refill?"

I caught the waiter's eye and gave him the sign.

She carried on. "Then Sunday, the news about Corey Brigham—of course that made it worse. And then yesterday, with Nero Wolfe again—you know how that was. And all day today, detectives and district attorneys with all of us—they were there all morning, and we have been at the district attorney's office all afternoon, in separate rooms. Now I have to tell it, I know that, but I don't think they'll believe me. I'm sure they won't. But they will if you say you went with me and saw me throw it in the river."

The waiter was coming with the refills, and I waited until he had gone.

"You left out something," I told her. "You left out about hiring a crew of divers to search the river bottom and offering a trip to Hollywood and ten thousand dollars in cash to the one who found the gun."

She surveyed me. "Are you being droll?"

"Not very. But that would give it color and would stand up just as well. Since you've been answering questions all day, I suppose you have accounted for your movements Thursday morning. What did you tell them?"

She nodded. "I'll have to admit I lied, I know that. I told them that after breakfast I was on the terrace until about half past eleven, and then I went shopping, and then I went to lunch on the *Bolivar*. Now I'll have to admit I didn't go shopping."

"Where did you tell them you went?"

"To three shoe shops."

"Did you name the shops?"

"Yes. They asked. Zussman's, and Yorio's, and Weeden's."

"Did you buy any shoes?"

228

"Yes, I—" She chopped it off. "Of course not, if I wasn't there. How could I?"

I shook my head at her. "Drink up. What was the name of the girl who hung onto the clapper so the bell couldn't ring, or was it a boy?"

"Damn it, don't be droll!"

"I'm not. You are. Beyond remarking that they'll check at those three shops, and that if you tried that mess on them they'd find that you didn't get your car from the garage that morning, there's no point in listing the dozen or so other holes. I should be sore at you for thinking I could be sap enough to play with you, but you meant well, and it's a tough trick to be both noble and nimble. So drink up and forget it—unless you want to tell me who *did* take the gun. Do you know?"

"Of course I don't!"

"Just protecting the whole bunch, including Nora?"

"I'm not protecting anybody! I just want this awful business to stop!" She touched my hand with fingertips. "Archie. So I made a mess of it, but it wouldn't be a mess if you would help me work it out. We could have done it Wednesday night. We didn't take my car, we took a taxi—or we walked to the East River and threw it in. Won't you help me?"

And there you are. What if I had lost sight of basic facts? The circumstances had been favorable. When I first saw her Monday afternoon on the terrace, as she approached with the sun full on her, I had realized that no alterations were needed anywhere, from the top of her head clear down to her toes. Talking with her, I had realized that she was fine company. At Colonna's Tuesday evening I had realized that she was good to be close to. Not to mention that by the time I was too old to provide for the family her father would have died and left her a mint. What if I had lost my head, made a supreme effort, rushed her off her feet, and wrapped her up? I would now be stuck with a female who got so rattled in a pinch that she thought she could sidetrack a murder investigation with a plant so half-baked it was pathetic. There you are.

But she meant well, so I let her down easy, paid for the drinks without entering it on my expense pad, helped her into a taxi, and had no hard feelings as I took another one, to 20th Street.

Nothing doing on the reports. Neither

230

Cramer nor Stebbins was around, and all Rowcliff had for me was a glassy eye.

As I said, Cramer didn't shake loose until noon the next day, Wednesday. I lunched on sandwiches and milk at a desk he let me use, digging out what was wanted, got home with it at four o'clock and got at the typewriter, and had just finished and was putting the original and a carbon on Wolfe's desk when he came down from the plant rooms. He got arranged in his chair, picked up the original, and started his brain exercise. I give it here, from the original from the Jarrell file, not for you to exercise your brain—unless you insist on it—but for the record.

May 29 1957
AG for NW

JARRELL TIMETABLES

(Mostly from police reports, but some from AG is included. Comments are AG's. Some items have been firmly verified by police, some partly verified, some not yet verified at all. Too complicated to try to distinguish among them, but can supply information on items considered important from my notes. OJ is Otis Jarrell, TJ is his wife, WJ is Wyman Jarrell, SJ is his wife, LJ is Lois Jarrell, NK is Nora Kent, RF is Roger Foote, AG is either Alan Green or Archie Goodwin, depending.)

OTIS JARRELL

Thursday

9:30 breakfast with WJ, LJ, NK, AG, then in library until lunch at 1:30 with TJ, SJ, & AG. Left at 2:30 for three business appointments: (1) Continental Trust Co., 287 Madison Ave., (2) Lawrence H. Eggers, 630 5th Ave., (3) Paul Abramowitz, 250 Park Ave. Exact times on these being checked. Got home at 6:00, went to his room. At 6:30 cocktails and dinner, then to library; AG joins him there at 10:35 p.m. Bed.

Friday

8:15 to AG's room to tell him Eber killed. 8:45 breakfast. 9:30 gathers everyone in library for conference about Eber. At 11:00 Lieut. Rowcliff comes, stays an hour, NK is present. Stays in library with WJ & NK; at 1:22 phone call comes from AG; at 1:40 calls AG, is told to bring everyone to NW office at 6:00. 1:45 lunch with SJ, LJ, & RF, tells them to be at NW office at 6:00. After lunch phones WJ and Corey Brigham to tell them. Phones Clarinda Day's & leaves word for TJ to call him. She does at 3:00 & he tells her about NW summons. Phones district attorney, whom he knows, & has friendly talk about Eber. 5:00 RF comes to library, asks for $335, doesn't get it. 5:30 is ready to leave for NW, waits until 5:50 for TJ to be ready. 6:10 arrives NW, leaves 7:10; home, dinner, long family discussion of situation, bed.

Saturday

8:30 breakfast with NK. Has everyone told to stand by because asst. DA coming at 11:00. 9:15 Herman Dietz comes on business matter, leaves at 9:45. 10:00 tells AG to make himself scarce because asst. DA coming. 10:10 WJ comes in for talk. 11:00 Mandelbaum arrives with dick stenographer; 11:15 everybody is called in, except that TJ doesn't make it until 11:45. 12:05 Cramer joins them, having just left NW. 1:35 Mandelbaum and Cramer leave. All lunch together except NK. 2:45 phones DA, can't get him.

Phones Police Commissioner Kelly and arranges to meet him at Penguin Club at 10:30 Sunday. 3:40 leaves to meet WJ at Metropolitan Athletic Club for talk. 5:40 they go home together for early dinner. 8:10 to theater with TJ.

Sunday
9:00 breakfast. 10:10 leaves for Penguin Club for date with Police Commissioner Kelly, with him until 11:30, goes home & to library. 12:00 AG comes in and stays 10 minutes. 1:30 lunch with WJ, SJ, & AG. 2:30 to 5:00 in library, then bridge with TJ, WJ, & NK. At 6:10 AG comes to announce Corey Brigham's death.

TRELLA JARRELL

Thursday
Up at noon, coffee on terrace. 1:30 lunch with OJ, SJ, & AG. 2:30 to Clarinda Day's. 3:45 shopping, information about where & when confused & incomplete & being checked. 6:00 home to change for cocktails & dinner. After dinner, pinochle with RF & NK.

Friday

9:30 goes to family conference in library in negligee, returns to bed, up at noon, eats big breakfast. 1:15 goes to park, arrives 2:30 at Clarinda Day's, gets message to call OJ, does so at 3:00. 4:00 to 5:00 looks at cats in two pet shops, gets home at 5:15, ready to leave for NW at 5:50. From there on with others as under OJ.

Saturday

Told at 11:05 to come to library to join party with asst. DA, makes it at 11:45. 1:35 lunch with others. 2:30 to Clarinda Day's. 3:45 to movie at Duke's Screen Box on Park Avenue. 5:30 home to dress for early dinner. 8:10 to theater with OJ.

Sunday

Up at noon, big breakfast again. On terrace with papers. 2:00 went to park, back at 3:00, went to studio to watch television, is wakened by WJ at 5:00 for bridge with OJ, WJ, & NK. At 6:10 AG announces Corey Brigham's death.

Thursday

9:30 breakfast with OJ, LJ, NK, & AG. 10:30 to 12:15, on terrace reading play in manuscript. 12:45 arrives at Sardi's and has lunch with three men to discuss financing of play he may produce (two of them have verified it). 2:45 to 4:30, auditions for casting play at Drew Theatre. 4:35 to 6:30 at Metropolitan Athletic Club, watching handball & drinking. 6:45 meets Susan at Sardi's, dinner, theater, home, bed.

Friday

9:30 family conference in library, then breakfast. Reads papers, waits around with SJ until Rowcliff has come & gone. In library with OJ & NK until 1:22, when phone call comes from AG; leaves, cashes check at bank, then to his office in Paramount Bldg. Lunch at Sardi's with same three men as on Thursday. 3:00 back to his office, gets call from OJ telling him to be at NW office at 6:00. Gets call from SJ. 3:45 SJ comes for him in Jaguar, they drive up to Briscoll's in Westchester for a drink, then back to town, arriving NW at 5:56. From there on with others under OJ.

Saturday

9:10 breakfast with SJ, LJ, & AG. 10:10 in library with OJ until 11:00, when asst. DA arrives. 1:35 lunch with others. 3:00 meets Corey Brigham at Churchill men's bar, with him until 3:50. 4:00 to 5:40 with OJ at Metropolitan Athletic Club; they go home together, arriving at 6:00 for early dinner. 8:15 to theater with SJ.

Sunday

10:00 breakfast with SJ, LJ, NK, & AG. Reads papers and does crossword puzzles until 1:30 lunch with OJ, SJ, & AG. 2:40 leaves for Drew Theatre to hear auditions. 4:40 leaves theater, gets home at 5:00, goes to studio and wakes TJ, bridge with OJ, TJ, & NK. At 6:10 AG announces Corey Brigham's death.

SUSAN JARRELL

Thursday

10:30 breakfast alone. To Masson's, jeweler, 52nd & 5th Ave., to leave watch. Walks to park & in park, then home at

1:30 for lunch with OJ, TJ, & AG. 2:45 back to Masson's to get watch; buys stockings at Merrihew's, 58th & Madison. Arrives Clarinda Day's at 4:00, leaves at 6:30, meets WJ at Sardi's at 6:45. Dinner, theater, home, bed.

Friday
9:30 family conference in library, then breakfast. Waits around with WJ until Rowcliff has come & gone. 12:10 goes to Abingdon's, florist at 65th & Madison, to order plants for terrace. Back home. 1:45 lunch with OJ, LJ, & RF, is told to be at NW office at 6:00. Rings WJ's office three times, gets him at 3:20, gets Jaguar and goes for him. Rest of day & evening, corroborates WJ.

Saturday
9:10 breakfast with WJ, LJ, & AG. On terrace until 11:15, joins party in library with asst. DA. 1:35 lunch with others. 2:45 goes to Abingdon's to look at plants. Home at 3:45, in room until 4:40, leaves, arrives Clarinda Day's 5:05, leaves at 6:15, is late at home for early dinner. 8:15 to theater with WJ.

Sunday

10:00 breakfast with WJ, LJ, NK, & AG. 10:30 leaves for St. Thomas Church, 53rd & 5th Ave. After church walks home, arriving 1:15. 1:30 lunch with OJ, WJ, & AG. Reads papers, looks at television, goes to room and takes nap, back to television at 5:30, is there with AG at 6:00 when news comes about Corey Brigham.

LOIS JARRELL

Thursday

9:30 breakfast with OJ, WJ, NK, & AG. 10:15 to 11:30 on terrace reading. 11:45 to 1:00 buying shoes at three shops: Zussman's, Yorio's and Weeden's. Bought seven pairs altogether, not liking to go barefoot. 1:15 lunch at party on steamship *Bolivar* at dock in Hudson River. 3:00 got car from garage & drove to Net Club in Riverdale, tennis until 6:00. Home at 6:35 to change. Left at 7:30 for dinner and dancing with a group at Flamingo Club; wish I had been there.

Friday

Up at 7:00 for breakfast & ride on a horse in park. Home just in time for family conference in library at 9:30. Drives to Net Club for an hour of tennis, home at 1:15. 1:45 lunch with OJ, SJ, & RF, is told to be at NW office at 6:00. 3:00 to Evangeline's, 49th Street near Madison, to try on clothes. Home at 5:20, leaves at 5:30 with RF & NK to taxi to NW. From there on with others as under OJ.

Saturday

Up at 7:00 to ride in park, back for breakfast at 9:10 with WJ, SJ, & AG. Cancels tennis date because of party in library with asst. DA at 11:15. 1:35 lunch with others. 2:30 takes nap in her room. 4:15 goes for walk, goes to Abingdon's & cancels Susan's order for plants for terrace. Home at 5:45, dresses for early dinner. 8:20 goes with AG to Flamingo Club, home at 2:00 a.m.

Sunday

10:00 breakfast with WJ, SJ, NK, & AG. Goes for walk with AG, at 11:30 takes taxi to apartment of friends named Buchanan, 185 East River Drive, goes with them to Net Club for lunch, tennis, drinks. Home at 6:40, learns about Corey Brigham.

Thursday

9:30 breakfast with OJ, WJ, LJ, & AG. Library all morning, lunch alone there, remains there alone until OJ returns at 6:00. After cocktails & dinner, pinochle with TJ & RF.

Friday

8:45 breakfast. 9:30 family conference in library. 11:00 with OJ when Rowcliff comes. Lunches in library, learns caliber of bullet that killed Eber, leaves at 1:45 to go to see NW. Home at 3:10, in library until 5:30, leaves with LJ & RF to go to the meeting at NW. From there on with others as under OJ.

Saturday

8:30 breakfast with OJ, then with him to library. 10:10 WJ comes for talk with OJ & she is told to beat it. In her room until 11:15, when she joins party in library with asst. DA. 1:35 lunch with others. 2:30 back to library with OJ; he leaves at 3:40. 3:45 gets phone call from Abingdon's about plants; she goes and cancels orders given by both SJ & LJ. Goes shopping, buys various personal items not specified. 5:45 gets home, dresses for early dinner. 7:50 leaves for meeting of Professional Women's League at Vassar Club, 58th Street. Home at 11:10.

Sunday
10:00 breakfast with WJ, SJ, LJ, & AG. 10:50 goes to church at 5th Ave. Presbyterian, 55th St. Lunch at Borgner's on 6th Ave., then to Picasso show at Modern Museum, 53rd St. Home at 5:00 for bridge with OJ, TJ, & WJ. At 6:10 AG announces Corey Brigham's death.

ROGER FOOTE

Thursday
7:00 breakfast alone. To Jamaica race track, loses $60 I lent him, home at 6:00. After cocktails and dinner, pinochle with TJ & NK.

Friday
9:30 family conference in library, then breakfast. On terrace & in his room until 1:45, then lunch with OJ, SJ, & LJ, is told to be at NW office at 6:00. 2:50 leaves to go to 49th Street to see if he can

242

get into Eber's apartment to look for a record, if any, of the fact that he owed Eber $335. No luck, apartment sealed. Calls on a lawyer he knows, unnamed, to find out where he stands. Gets home at 5:00, goes to library to try to borrow $335 from OJ, is turned down. 5:30 leaves with LJ & NK for NW office.

Saturday

10:15 breakfast alone. 11:15 joines party with asst. DA in library. 1:35 lunch with others. 2:45 goes to Mitchell's Riding Academy on West 108th Street to look at a horse. 3:45 returns home and plays solitaire in his room until time for early dinner. After dinner invites AG to play gin, AG declines. Goes to bed at 9:00.

Sunday

7:00 breakfast alone. To Belmont race track to look at horses. Home at 7:00 p.m., learns about Corey Brigham. Has given police details of his day at Belmont, but they are too confused & complicated to be worth copying.

——15———

At a quarter past ten Thursday morning, Memorial Day, I arrived at Jamaica race track to start the damnedest four days of detecting, or non-detecting, that I have ever put in.

After Wolfe had picked up the time-tables, at six o'clock Wednesday, he had read them in twenty minutes, and then had gone over them for more than an hour, until dinner time. Back in the office after dinner, he had asked a few dozen questions. What did I know about Mr. and Mrs. Herman Dietz? Practically nothing. Had Trella Jarrell's hour in the park from two o'clock to three on Sunday been checked? No, and probably it never would be. If I wanted to leave a revolver in Central Park where I was reasonably certain it wouldn't be discovered for three days, but where I could get it when I wanted it, where would I hide it? I made three suggestions, none of them any good, and said I'd have to think it over.

Who was Clarinda Day? She was a woman who ran an establishment on 48th Street just off Fifth Avenue where women could get almost anything done that occurred to them—to their hair, their faces, their necks, their busts, their waists, their hips, their legs, their knees, their calves, their ankles—and where they could sweat, freeze, rest, or exercise forty-two different ways. Her customers ran all the way from stenographers to multi-millionairesses.

Did Nora Kent have keys to all the files in Jarrell's library and the combination to the safes? Don't know. Had a thorough search been made of the Jarrell duplex? Yes; a regiment of experts, with Jarrell's permission, had spent all day Tuesday at it. Including the library? Yes, with Jarrell present. Who told me so? Purley Stebbins. Where was the Metropolitan Athletic Club? Central Park South, 59th Street. How long would it take to get from where the steamship *Bolivar* was docked to Eber's apartment on 49th Street? Between ten and thirty minutes, depending on traffic. Average, say eighteen minutes. How difficult would it have been for Nora Kent to get from the library to the street, and, later, back in again, without being observed? With luck, using the service entrance, fairly simple. Without luck, impossible.

Etc.

At ten thirty Wolfe leaned back and said, "Instructions."

"Yes, sir."

"Before you go to bed get Saul, Fred, and Orrie, and ask them to be here at eleven in the morning."

"Yes, sir."

"Tomorrow is a holiday. I don't suppose Miss Bonner will be at her office. If possible, get her tonight and ask her to breakfast with me at eight."

I looked at him. He meant business, though what business I couldn't say. Add his opinion of women to his opinion of other detectives, and you get his opinion of female detectives. Circumstances had compelled him to use Dol Bonner a year or so back, but now he was asking for it, and even inviting her to breakfast. Fritz would be on needles.

"I have her home number," I told him, "and I'll try, but she may already be gone for the long week end. If so, is it urgent enough to dig her out?"

"Yes. I want her. Now for you. You will

go early in the morning to Jamaica race track and—"

"No racing at Jamaica now. It's closed."

"What about Belmont?"

"Open. Big day tomorrow."

"Then we'll see. You will act on this hypothesis: that Roger Foote took Jarrell's gun and hid it in his room or elsewhere on the premises. Thursday afternoon he shot Eber with it. Since he intended to say he had spent the day at Jamaica, he went there so as to be seen, and he hid the gun somewhere there. To speculate as to why he hid it instead of disposing of it is pointless; we know he did hide it because it was used again on Sunday. Either he hid it at Jamaica or, having made an appearance there, he went to Belmont and hid it there. In either case, on Sunday he went and retrieved it, returned to New York, met Brigham by appointment, and killed him. Acting on that hypothesis, your job is to learn where he left the gun from Thursday to Sunday, and you may start either at Jamaica or at Belmont. It's barely possible you'll even find the gun. He may have thought he might have further use for it and went back and hid it again in the same place after killing Brigham. He didn't get home Sunday until seven o'clock."

I said—not an objection, just a fact—"Of course, he had all of New York City too."

"I know, but that's hopeless. He had to go to Jamaica on Thursday and to Belmont on Sunday, to be seen, and since we know he was there we'll look there. We know little or nothing of his movements in New York City; we know of no place particularly available to him where he could hide a gun and count on getting it again. First explore the possibilities at Jamaica and Belmont."

I explored them for four straight days, equipped with five hundred bucks in small bills from cash reserve and eight pictures of Roger Foote, procured early Thursday morning from the files at the *Gazette*. I went to Jamaica first because Belmont would have such a mob on the holiday that I would merely have got trampled.

Meanwhile, throughout the four days, Wolfe presumably had the gang busy working on other hypotheses—including Dol Bonner—though he never told me who was after what, except that I gathered Saul Panzer was on Otis Jarrell himself. That was a compliment to the former client, since Saul's rate was sixty bucks a day and expenses and he was worth at least five times that. Fred Durkin was good but no Saul

Panzer. Orrie Cather, whom you have seen at my desk, was yes and no. On some tricks he was unbeatable, but on others not so hot. As for Dol Bonner, I didn't know much about her firsthand, but the word around was that if you had to have a female dick she was it. She had her own office and a staff—with one of which, Sally Colt, I was acquainted.

By Sunday night I knew enough about Jamaica and Belmont, especially Belmont, to write a book, with enough left over for ten magazine articles. I knew four owners, nine trainers, seventeen stable boys, five jockeys, thirteen touts, twenty-eight miscellaneous characters, one lamb, three dogs, and six cats, to speak to. I had aroused the suspicions of two track dicks and become close friends with one. I had seen two hundred and forty-seven girls it would have been fun to talk to but was too busy. I had seen about the same number of spots where a gun could be hid, but could find no one who had seen Roger Foote near any of them. None of them held a gun at the time I called, nor could I detect any trace of oil or other evidence that a gun had been there. One of them, a hole in a tree the other side of the backstretch, was so ideal that I was tempted to hide my own gun in it. Another good place would have been the bottom of a rack outside Gallant Man's stall, but there were too many eagle eyes around. Peach Fuzz wasn't there.

Sunday night I told Wolfe there was nothing left to explore unless he wanted me to start looking in horse's mouths, and he said he would have new instructions in the morning.

But he never gave them to me, for a little after ten on Monday a call came inviting me to visit the DA's office, and, after buzzing Wolfe in the plant rooms to tell him where to find me, I went. After thirty minutes with Mandelbaum and a dick I knew one thing, that the several hundred city and county employes working in the case had got exactly as far as I had at Jamaica and Belmont. After another thirty minutes I knew another thing, that the police commissioner and the district attorney had decided it had become necessary to find out what I was doing at Jarrell's under an assumed name, no matter how Jarrell felt about it. I said I wanted to phone Mr. Wolfe and was told that all the phones were busy. At noon I was taken in to the DA himself and had forty minutes with him that did neither of us any good. At one o'clock I was allowed to take my pick of ham or turkey in a sandwich; no corned beef. I insisted on milk and got it. At two-thirty I decided it had gone far enough and was walking out, but was stopped. Held as a material witness. Then, of course, they had to let me make a phone call, and within minutes there was a call for Mandelbaum from Nathaniel Parker, who is Wolfe's lawyer when Wolfe is driven to the extremity of using one.

I didn't get locked up at all. The DA had another try at me and then sent me into another room with a dick named O'Leary, and in two hours I won $3.12 from him at gin. I was perfectly willing to give him a chance to get it back, but someone came and took me to Mandelbaum's room, and Nathaniel Parker was there. As I shook hands with him Mandelbaum warned me not to leave the jurisdiction, and I said I wanted it in writing, and he said to go to hell, and I said I didn't know that was in the jurisdiction, and Parker steered me out.

Down on the sidewalk I asked him, "How high am I priced this time?"

"No bail, Archie. No warrant. I persuaded Mandelbaum that the circumstances didn't call for it, and promised that you will be available when needed."

I was a little disappointed because being out on bail is good for the ego. It gives you a sense of importance, of being wanted; it makes you feel that people care. However, I didn't reproach Parker; he had acted for the best. We took a taxi together uptown, but he said he had a dinner appointment and didn't get out when we reached the old brownstone on West 35th Street. So I thanked him for the rescue and the lift. As I crossed the sidewalk to the stoop my wrist watch said 6:23.

Wolfe, at his desk reading a book, lifted his eyes to grunt a greeting and returned them to the book. I went to my desk to see if there were any memos for me, found none, sat, and inquired, "Anything happen?"

He said no, without looking up.

"Parker said to give you his regards. I am not under bail. He talked Mandelbaum out of it."

He grunted.

"They've decided that Jarrell's private affairs are no longer private. They'll be after you any time, in the morning at the latest. Do you want a report?"

He said no, without looking up.

"Any instructions?"

He lifted his eyes, said, "I'm reading, Archie," and lowered them back to the book.

The best thing to throw at him would have been the typewriter, but I didn't own it. Next best would have been the telephone, but I didn't own that, either, and the cord wasn't long enough. I got up and left, mounted the two flights to my room, showered, decided not to shave, put on a clean shirt and a lighter suit, and was sewing buttons on pajamas when Fritz called up that dinner was ready.

It was at the table that I caught on that something was up. Wolfe wasn't being crusty because the outlook was dark; he was being smug because he had tasted blood, or was expecting to. He always enjoyed his food, whether in spite of circumstances or in harmony with them, and after ten thousand meals with him I knew all the shades. The way he spread pâté on a cracker, the way he picked up the knife to slice the filet of beef in aspic, the way he used his fork on the salad, the way he made his choice from the cheese platter—no question about it, he had something or somebody by the tail, or at least the tail was in sight.

I was thinking that when we were back in the office with coffee he might think it was time to let me have a taste too, but no. After taking three sips he picked up his book. That was a little too much, and I was deciding whether to go after him head on or take him from the flank, when the doorbell rang and I went to answer it. In view of Wolfe's behavior I wouldn't have been surprised if it had been the whole gang, all seven of them, with a joint confession in triplicate signed and ready to deliver, but it was merely a middle-aged man in a light brown suit and no hat whom I had never seen before.

When I opened the door he spoke before I did. "Is this Nero Wolfe's house?"

"Right."

"Are you Archie Goodwin?"

"Right again."

"Okay." He extended a hand with a little package. "This is for Nero Wolfe."

I took it and he turned and was going. I told him to wait, but he called over his shoulder, "No receipt," and kept going. I looked at the package. It was the size of a box of kitchen matches, wrapped in brown paper, fastened with Scotch tape, and if it bore any name of address it was in invisible ink.

I shut the door and returned to the office and told Wolfe, "The man who handed me this said it was for you, but I don't know how he knew. There's no name on it. It doesn't tick. Shall I open it under water?"

"As you please. It's hardly large enough to be dangerous."

That seemed optimistic, remembering the size of the capsule that had once exploded in that office inside a metal percolator, blowing the percolator lid at the wall, missing Wolfe's head by an inch. However, I could stand it if he could. I got out my knife to cut the tape, removed the paper wrapping, and disclosed a cardboard box with no label. Putting it on the desk midway between us, which was only fair, I eased the lid off. Cotton. I lifted the cotton, and there was more cotton, with an object resting in its center. Bending over for a close-up, I straightened and announced, "A thirty-eight bullet. Isn't that interesting?"

"Extremely." He reached for the box and gave it a look. "Very interesting. You're sure it's a thirty-eight?"

"Yes, sir. Quite a coincidence."

"It is indeed." He put the box down. "Who brought it?'

"A stranger. Too bad I didn't invite him in."

"Yes. Of course there are various possibilities—among them, that some prankster sent it."

"Yeah. So I toss it in the wastebasket?"

"I don't think so. There is at least one other possibility that can't be ignored. You've had a long day and I dislike asking it, but you might take it to Mr. Cramer, tell him how we got it, and suggest that it be compared with the bullets that killed Mr. Eber and Mr. Brigham."

"Uh-huh. In time, say in a week or so, that might have occurred to me myself. My mind's not as quick as yours." I replaced the top layer of cotton and put the lid on. "I'd better take the wrapping paper too. If the bullet matches, and it just might, he'll want it. Incidentally, he'll want me too. If I take him a thirty-eight bullet, with that suggestion, and with that story of how we got it, I'll have to shoot my way out if you want to see me again tonight."

"The devil." He was frowning. "You're quite right. That won't do." He thought a moment. "Your notebook. A letter to Mr. Cramer."

I got at my desk and took notebook and pen.

He dictated: "Dear Mr. Cramer. I send you herewith a package which was delivered at my door a few minutes ago. It bore no name or address, but the messenger told Mr. Goodwin it was for me and departed. It contains a bullet which Mr. Goodwin says is a thirty-eight. Doubtless it is merely a piece of tomfoolery, but I thought it best to send it to you. You may think it worth while to have the bullet compared with those that killed Mr. Eber and Mr. Brigham. Then discard it. Don't bother to return it. Sincerely."

"By mail?" I asked.

"No. Take it, please. Immediately. Hand it in and return at once."

"Glad to." I pulled the typewriter around.

—16—

THAT Monday night may not have been the worst night Fritz ever spent, for he has had some tough ones, but it was bad enough. When I had got back after delivering the package at 20th Street, a little after ten o'clock, Wolfe had called him to the office.

"Some instructions, Fritz."

"Yes, sir."

"Archie and I will go up to bed shortly, but we are not here and will not be here. You will answer the phone. You do not know where we are or when we will return. You do not know exactly when we left. You may be bullyragged, by Mr. Cramer or others, but you will maintain that position. You will take messages if any are given, to be delivered to us when we return. You will ignore the doorbell. You will open no outside door, stoop or basement or back, under any circumstances whatever. If you do, a search warrant may be thrust at you and the house will be overrun. A contingency might arise that will make you consider it necessary to disturb Archie or me, but I think not and hope not. Bring my breakfast an hour early, at seven o'clock. Archie will have his at seven also. I shall be sorry if you fail of a proper night's sleep, but it can't be helped. You can take a nap tomorrow."

"Yes, sir." Fritz swallowed. "If there is any danger, may I suggest—" He stopped and started over. "I know you are reluctant to leave the house, that is understood, but there are times when it is better to leave a house, at least for a short time. Especially in your profession." He looked at me. "You know that, Archie."

Wolfe assured him, "No, Fritz, there is no danger. On the contrary, this is the pre-amble to triumph. You understand the instructions?"

He said he did, but he wasn't happy. For years he had been expecting the day to come when Wolfe would be dragged out of the house in handcuffs, not to mention me, and he was against it. He gave me a reproachful look, which God knows I didn't deserve, and left, and Wolfe and I, not being there anyway, went up to bed.

Seven o'clock is much too early a breakfast hour unless you're a bird or a bird watcher, but I made it to the kitchen by 7:08. My glass of orange juice was there, but Fritz wasn't, and the phone was ringing. It was a temptation to take it and see how well I could imitate Fritz's voice, but I let it ring. By the time Fritz came it had given up. I told him he must have been late taking Wolfe's breakfast tray up, and he said no, he had got it there on the dot at seven, but had stayed to report on the night.

While I dealt with toast, bacon, fresh

strawberry omelet, and coffee, he reported to me, referring to notes. The first call from Lieutenant Rowcliff had come at 11:32, and he had been so emphatic that Fritz had hung up on him. The second had been at 11:54, less emphatic but stubborner. At 12:21 Cramer had called, and had got both personal and technical, explaining the penalties that could be imposed on a man, Fritz for instance, for complicity in withholding evidence and obstructing justice in a murder investigation. At 12:56 the doorbell had started to ring, and at 1:03 pounding on the front door had begun. From 1:14 to a little after six peace had reigned, but at 6:09 Cramer had phoned, and at 6:27 the doorbell had started up again, and through the one-way glass panel Sergeant Stebbins had been visible. He had kept at it for five minutes and was now in a police car with a colleague out at the curb.

I got up, went to the front door for a look, came back, requested more toast, and poured more coffee. "He's still there," I told Fritz, "and there's one danger. As you know, Mr. Wolfe can't bear the idea of a hungry man in his house, and while Stebbins isn't actually in the house he's there in front and wants to be, and he looks hungry. If

260

Mr. Wolfe sees him and suspects he hasn't had breakfast there'll be hell to pay. Could I borrow a little wild thyme honey?"

I was on the last bite of toast and honey and the last inch of coffee when the sound of Wolfe's elevator came, and by the time I was through swallowing and got to the office he was there behind his desk. We said good morning.

"So," I said, "it wasn't a prankster."

"Apparently not." With the edge of a blotter he was flipping from his desk pad dust that wasn't there. "Get Mr. Cramer."

I got the phone and dialed, and soon had him, and Wolfe took it. I held my receiver an inch from my ear, expecting a blast, but it had gone beyond that. Cramer's voice was merely hoarse with fury.

"Where are you?" he demanded.

"I'm on an errand, no matter where. I'm calling to ask about the bullet I sent you. Does it match the others?"

"You know damn well it does. You knew it when you sent it. This is the rawest—"

"No. I suspected it, but I didn't know it. That was what I had to know before I divulged where it came from. That was why I arranged to keep its source anonymous until I knew. I would like to have it explicitly.

261

Was the bullet I sent you fired from the same gun as those that killed Eber and Brigham?"

"By God." Cramer knew darned well he shouldn't use profanity on the phone, so he must have been upset. "You arranged! I'll arrange you! I'll arrange for you to—"

"Mr. Cramer! This is ridiculous. I'm supplying the solution of an extremely bothersome case, and you sputter at me. If you must sputter, wait until you have the facts. Will you please answer my question?"

"The answer is yes."

"Then I'm ready to deliver the murderer and the weapon, but there is the matter of procedure to consider. I can invite the district attorney to my house and give him the weapon and two excellent witnesses, and let him get the culprit. Or I can do that with you. I don't like either of those because I have been at considerable expense and I have earned a fee, and I want to be paid, and there is plenty of money in that family. I want the family to know what I have done, and how, and the most effective and impressive way to inform them is to have them present when I produce the weapon and identify the murderer. If I invite them they won't come. You can bring them. If you'll—please let me finish. If you'll have them at my house at eleven o'clock, all of them, I'll be there to receive you, and you'll get all you need and more. Three hours from now. I hope you'll oblige me because I like dealing with you better than with the district attorney."

"I ought to appreciate that," Cramer said, hoarser than ever. "You're home now. You've been home all night. You knew damn well the bullet would match, and you knew as soon as we checked it we'd be on you, and you didn't want to be bothered until morning so you could spring this on me. In half an hour we'll have a search warrant for your house, and we'll have warrants for you and Goodwin as material witnesses."

"Indeed. Then forgive me if I ring off. I have a call to make."

"Yeah. You would. By God, you would. I let you have those reports and this is what I get for it. Who do you want there?"

"The five people named Jarrell, and Miss Kent and Mr. Foote. At eleven o'clock."

"Sure, I know. Until eleven you'll be up with your goddamn orchids. We mustn't interfere with that."

He hung up. So did we.

"You know," I said, "I think the orchids

irritate him. I've noticed it before. Maybe you should get rid of them. Do I answer the phone now?"

"Yes. Miss Bonner and Saul and Fred and Orrie are going to call between nine and nine-thirty. Tell them to come at eleven. If the Jarrells are to be properly impressed they should see all of them."

"Okay. But it wouldn't hurt if I knew in advance which one to keep an eye on. I know darned well it's not Roger Foote."

He looked up at the wall clock. "It's early. Very well."

—17——

I had turned over the doorman-and-usher job to Saul and Orrie because I was otherwise engaged. Cramer, with Stebbins, had arrived twenty minutes early and insisted on seeing Wolfe, and I had taken them to the dining room and stayed to keep them company. They didn't want my company, they wanted Wolfe's, but I told them that if they climbed three flights to the plant rooms they would find the door locked. I offered to pass the time by telling them the story about the chorus girl and the anteater, but it didn't seem to appeal to them.

When Wolfe opened the dining-room door and said, "Good morning, gentlemen," and Cramer told him to come in and shut the door, a wrangle seemed unavoidable, but Wolfe avoided it by saying, "In the office, please," and turning and going. Cramer and Stebbins followed, and I brought up the rear.

On the three previous occasions that Otis Jarrell had been in that office he had had the seat of honor, the red leather chair, but this time Saul, following instructions, had kept it for Inspector Cramer, and the ex-client was in the front row of the audience with his wife, his son, and his daughter-in-law. Behind them were Lois, Nora Kent, Roger Foote, and Saul Panzer. On the couch, at my back when I got to my desk, were Sally Colt, of Dol Bonner's staff, and Fred Durkin and Orrie Cather. Purley Stebbins' chair was where he always put it himself if we didn't, against the wall at arm's length from Cramer.

Actually, for that particular party, the red leather chair was not the seat of honor. The seat of honor was one of the yellow chairs which had been placed at the other end of

Wolfe's desk, on his right, and in it was Dol Bonner, a very attractive sight for a female dick, with her home-grown long black lashes making a curly canopy for her caramel-colored eyes. I had warned Fritz she would be there. She had once been invited to dine at the table he cooks for, and he suspects every woman who ever crosses the threshold of wanting to take over his kitchen, not to mention the rest of the house.

Inspector Cramer, standing, faced the audience and spoke. "Nero Wolfe is going to say something and you can listen along with me. You're here on police orders, so I want to make one thing clear. Any questions Wolfe asks you are his questions and not mine. Answer them or not as you please. Wolfe is not acting for the police or speaking for the police."

"I have nothing to ask, Mr. Cramer," Wolfe said. "Not a single question. I have only to report and expound."

"All right, go ahead." Cramer sat down.

"What I wish to report," Wolfe told the audience, "is how I found the weapon that killed two men, and how its finding revealed the identity of the killer. After you people left here on Monday, eight days ago, and after I had given Mr. Cramer the information I had told you I would give him, I was without a client and had no assigned function in this affair. But my curiosity was alive, my self-esteem was involved, and I wanted to be paid for the time I had spent and the ignominy I had endured. I resolved to pursue the matter."

He cleared his throat. "You people were no longer available to me for inquiry. You were through with me. I had neither the personnel nor the facilities for the various lines of routine investigation, and besides, the police were seeing to that. But there was one established fact that offered possibilities: the bullets that killed Eber and Brigham had been fired from the same gun. Assuming that they had also been fired by the same person, obviously the gun had been in his possession from Thursday afternoon, when Eber was killed, to Sunday afternoon, when Brigham was killed—or at least it had been kept where he could get it again. Where had it been kept?"

His eyes went to Cramer and back to them. "Mr. Cramer obliged me by permitting Mr. Goodwin access to the reports of your movements during that period. I was and am deeply appreciative of his cooperation; it would be churlish to suppose that he let me learn the contents of the reports only because he wanted to know what I was going to do with them. Here they are."

With a forefinger he tapped papers on his desk. "Here they are, as typed by Mr. Goodwin. I inspected and analyzed them. It was possible, of course, that the gun had been kept somewhere on the premises where you all live, but I thought it extremely unlikely. At any moment the police, learning of the disappearance of Mr. Jarrell's gun, might search the place—as they did eventually, one week ago today. It was highly probable that the gun had been kept somewhere else, and I proceeded on that theory."

"So did I," Cramer rasped.

Wolfe nodded. "No doubt. But for you it was only one of many lines of inquiry, whereas it was all I had. And not only was it a near-certainty that the gun had been kept in some available spot from Thursday afternoon to Sunday afternoon, but also there was a chance that it had been returned to that spot after Brigham was killed and was still there. On Sunday, when he left the car on Thirty-ninth Street, the murderer had the gun and had to dispose of it somehow. If he put it somewhere, anywhere, where it might be found, there was a risk that it *would* be found and would be identified both as Mr. Jarrell's gun and as the gun the bullets had come from. If he put it somewhere where it would *not* be found—for instance, at the bottom of the river—he might be seen, and besides, time was probably pressing. So it was quite possible that he had returned it, at the first opportunity, if not immediately, to the place where he had kept it for three days. Therefore my quest was for a spot not merely where the gun had been kept for the three days, but where it might still be."

He took a breath. "So I analyzed the timetables. They offered various suggestions, some promising, some far-fetched. To explore them I needed help, and I called on Mr. Saul Panzer, who is seated there beside Mr. Foote; on Mr. Fred Durkin, on the couch; on Mr. Orrie Cather, on the couch beside Mr. Durkin; on Miss Theodolinda Bonner, here at my right; and on Miss Sally Colt, Miss Bonner's assistant, on the couch beside Mr. Durkin."

"Get on with it," Cramer growled.

Wolfe ignored him. "I won't detail all their explorations, but some deserve brief mention. They were all severely handicapped by the holiday and the long week end. Mr.

Goodwin spent four days at the Jamaica and Belmont race tracks. Mr. Panzer traced Mr. Jarrell's movements on Thursday when Eber was killed with extraordinary industry and acumen. Mr. Durkin performed with perseverance and ingenuity at the Metropolitan Athletic Club. Mr. Cather found three different people who had seen Mrs. Jarrell in Central Park on the Sunday when Brigham was killed. But it was Miss Bonner and Miss Colt who had both ability and luck. Miss Bonner, produce the gun, please?"

Dol Bonner opened her bag, took out a revolver, said, "It's loaded," and put it on Wolfe's desk. Cramer came breezing around the front of the desk, nearly tripping on Wyman's foot, spouting as he came, and Purley Stebbins was up too. Dol Bonner told Cramer, "I tried it for prints, Inspector. There were no good ones. Look out, it's loaded."

"You loaded it?"

"No. It held two cases and four cartridges when I found it. I fired one cartridge, and that left—"

"You fired it?"

"Mr. Cramer," Wolfe said sharply. "How could we learn if it was the guilty gun without firing it? Let me finish and you can have all day."

I opened a drawer of my desk, got a heavy manila envelope, and handed it to Cramer. He picked the gun up by the trigger guard, put it in the envelope, circled Wolfe's desk to hand the envelope to Purley, said, "Go ahead and finish," and sat.

Wolfe asked, "What did you do after you found the gun, Miss Bonner?"

"Miss Colt was with me. We phoned you and got instructions and followed them. We went to my office and filed a nick in the barrel of the gun so we could identify it. We then went to my apartment, turned on the radio as loud as it would go, fired a bullet into some cushions, got the bullet, put it in a box with cotton, wrapped the box in paper, and sent it to you by messenger."

"When did you find the gun?"

"At ten minutes to six yesterday afternoon."

"Has it been continuously in your possession since then?"

"It has. Every minute. I slept with it under my pillow."

"Was Miss Colt with you when you found it?"

"Yes."

"Where did you find it?"

"In a locker on the fourth floor at Clarinda Day's on Forty-eighth Street."

Trella Jarrell let out a king-size gasp. Eyes went to her and she covered her mouth with both hands.

Wolfe went on. "Was the locker locked?"

"Yes."

"Did you break it open?"

"No. I used a key."

"I won't ask you how you got the key. You may be asked in court, but this is not a court. Was the locker one of a series?"

"Yes. There are four rows of private lockers on that floor, with twenty lockers to a row. Clarinda Day's customers put their clothes and belongings in them while they are doing exercises or getting massages. Some of them keep changes of clothing or other articles in them."

"You said private lockers. Is each locker confined to a single customer?"

"Yes. The customer has the only key, except that I suppose the management has a master key. The key I used—but I'm not to tell that now?"

"It isn't necessary. You may tell on the witness stand. As you know, what you did is actionable, but since you discovered a weapon that was used in two murders I doubt if you will suffer any penalty. Instead, you should be rewarded and probably will be. Do you know which of Clarinda Day's customers the locker belongs to? The one you found the gun in?"

"Yes. Mrs. Wyman Jarrell. Her name was on it. It also had other articles in it, and among them were letters in envelopes addressed to her."

No gasp from anyone. No anything, until Otis Jarrell muttered, barely loud enough to hear, "The snake, the snake."

Wolfe's eyes were on Susan. "Mrs. Jarrell. Do you wish to offer an explanation of how the gun got into your locker?"

Naturally, knowing what was coming, I had been watching her little oval face from a corner of my eye, and she was only four feet from me, and I swear there hadn't been a flicker. As she met Wolfe's eyes her lip muscles moved a little as if they were trying to manage a smile, but I had seen them do that before. And when she spoke it was the same voice, low, and shy or coy or wary or demure, depending on your attitude.

"I can't explain it," she said, "because I don't know. But you can't think I took it that day, that Wednesday, because I told you about that. I was upstairs in my room, and my husband was with me. Weren't you, Wy?"

She would probably have skipped that if she had turned for a good look at his face before asking it. He was paralyzed, staring at Wolfe with his jaw hanging. He looked incapable of speech, but a kind of idiot mumble came out, "I was taking a shower, a long shower, I always take a long shower."

You might think, when a man is hit so hard with the realization that his wife is a murderess that he lets something out which will help to sink her, he would at least give it some tone, some quality. That's a hell of a speech in a crisis like that: "I was taking a shower, a long shower. I always take a long shower."

As Wolfe would say, pfui.

——18————

As it turned out, when Otis Jarrell's private affairs, at least some of them, became public, it was out of his own mouth on the witness stand. While it was true that evidence of motive is not legally essential in a murder case, it helps a lot, and for that the

274

DA had to have Jarrell. The theory was that Susan had worked on Jim Eber and got information from him, specifically about the claim on the shipping company, and passed it along to Corey Brigham, who had acted on it. After Eber was fired he had learned about Brigham's clean-up on the deal, suspected he had been fired because Jarrell thought he had given the information to Brigham, remembered he had told Susan about it, suspected her of telling Brigham, and told her, probably just before I entered the studio that day, that he was going to tell Jarrell. To support the theory Jarrell was needed, though they had other items, the strongest one being that they found two hundred thousand dollars in cash in a safe-deposit box Susan had rented about that time, and she couldn't remember where she got it.

Brigham's death was out of it as far as the trial was concerned, since she was being tried for Eber, but the theory was that he had suspected her of killing Eber and had told her so, and take your pick. Either he had disapproved of murder so strongly that he was going to pass it on, or he wanted something for not passing it on—possibly the two hundred grand back, possibly something more personal.

None of the rest of them was called on to testify by either side. The defense put neither Susan nor Wyman on, and that probably hurt. Susan's having a key to the library was no problem, since her husband had one and she slept in the same room with him. As for whether they'll ever get her to the chair, you'll have to watch the papers. The jury convicted her of the big one, with no recommendation, but to get a woman actually in that seat, especially a young one with a little oval face, takes a lot of doing.

Wolfe took Jarrell's money, a check this time, and a very attractive one, and that's all right, he earned it. But that was all he wanted from that specimen, or me either. He said it for both of us the day after Susan was indicted, when Jarrell phoned to say he was going to mail a check for a certain amount and would that be satisfactory, and when Wolfe said it would Jarrell went on: "And I was right, Wolfe. She's a snake. You didn't believe me the day I came to hire you, and neither did Goodwin, but now you know I was right, and that gives me a lot of satisfaction. She's a snake."

"No, sir." Wolfe was curt. "I do not

know you were right. She is a murderess, a hellcat, and a wretch, but you have furnished no evidence that she is a snake. I still do not believe you. I will be glad to get the check."

He hung up and so did I.

The publishers hope that this
Large Print Book has brought
you pleasurable reading.
Each title is designed to make
the text as easy to see as possible.
G.K. Hall Large Print Books
are available from your library and
your local bookstore. Or, you can
receive information by mail on
upcoming and current Large Print Books
and order directly from the publishers.
Just send your name and address to:

G.K. Hall & Co.
70 Lincoln Street
Boston, Mass. 02111

or call, toll-free:

1-800-343-2806

A note on the text
Large print edition designed by
Kipling West.
Composed in 16 pt Plantin
on a Xyvision 300/Linotron 202N
by Stephen Traiger
of G.K. Hall & Co.